THE
TRUTH

JEFFRY W. JOHNSTON

sourcebooks
fire

Published by Sourcebooks Fire, an imprint of Sourcebooks, Inc.
P.O. Box 4410, Naperville, Illinois 60567-4410
(630) 961-3900
Fax: (630) 961-2168
www.sourcebooks.com

Library of Congress Cataloging-in-Publication data is on file with the publisher.

Printed and bound in the United States of America.
VP 10 9 8 7 6 5 4 3 2 1

For my son, Will.
Thank you for the inspiration.
Watching you grow up has been so much fun, and
the best years are yet to come.

1

NOW

I wake up to find I can't move, my arms and legs duct-taped tight to a wooden chair. Duct tape is also wrapped around my chest and the chair's hard, unyielding back.

The only thing not bound is my head, but I can only turn it left and right. I can't look behind me because of the chair's high back.

Christ, what is this!

My head hurts. I feel nauseous, dizzy. Can't focus. What happened? How did I get here? My memory's a blur.

"Hey!" I shout. "Hey! Anybody here?"

I wait a few seconds. Nothing.

I see unfinished walls, but I could be in a room any-where. The only furniture I can see is a metal folding chair leaning against the wall opposite.

Wait a minute! What about Devon? The last thing I remember was calling on my cell phone to make sure he got to the field okay. What time is it? Is he in the middle of his game, wondering where I am? Is Mom there, wondering the same thing?

I can tell my cell is not in my pocket, not that I'd be able to reach it anyway. Where is it? How long have I been out? A couple hours? A whole day? Is it still…what, Saturday? Are people looking for me? The police?

"Hey!" I shout again. "*Heeeyyyy!*" I try harder to break free. "Is somebody here? Can somebody help me? Please! *Please!*"

Who could have done this to me? Why?

"Help! Help me! *Heeelllp!*"

This isn't working. I need to calm down and try to think. *Come on, breathe. That's it. Again. Now another breath.* My heart is starting to slow a bit. That's good. Maybe closing my eyes will help.

Two more deep breaths. Okay. Now, think.

I remember dialing my cell. But before that, I had knocked on Rita's front door. We were going to go to Devon's game together. I was waiting for her to open the door. Wait, the door did start to open. Then... nothing. Or...something. Something made me pass out. Something with a sweet smell. Held against my face. Making me gag. Feel sick. I couldn't push it away. Something very strong was holding it in place.

Not some*thing*. Some*one*.

I hear movement. Behind me. A door opening. I try to look back. Can't.

The door closes. A quiet click.

Then footsteps. Steady, determined.

I recognize the guy who appears in front of me. Derek Brannick. Only a year older than me, which makes him seventeen, but with the broken front teeth and scar on his throat he looks much older.

He's holding something in his hand, which he slips into his pants pocket before I can see it. Then he picks up the metal chair from against the wall and opens it before straddling it and leaning over the back, facing me. He lowers his head. Does nothing for a couple minutes. My heart slams against my chest. I wait. So scared I can't think straight.

Finally, he raises his head and looks at me. His eyes... it's as if there's no light in them. Nothing. Dead eyes. "You want some water?" His voice is raspy. He stands and moves out of my field of vision. I hear a faucet turning on and off. Then he's back with a paper cup. "Tilt your head back," he says. I do the best I can. Some of the water runs down my chin, but enough makes it into my mouth. The water's lukewarm, but I welcome it.

"Feel better? Can you talk? 'Cause you're gonna need to be able to talk." He crumples the cup and throws it on the floor.

"Yes," I croak. "Th...thank you." My voice is trembling. I can't help it.

Derek nods, lets out another long breath as if he has the weight of the world on his shoulders, and sits back in his chair, pulling it closer to me.

"I'm...I'm sorry," I try. "I'm really—"

"Shh," he says sharply, pointing a finger at me. "I told you before, Chris...I'm not looking for that."

"I should have showed up at the—"

"Shhh!"

He begins to cough. It sounds painful. He starts to talk again, then stops. Maybe it's painful to talk too. The way his voice is all rough and raspy, it wouldn't surprise me.

Derek tries again. "I tied you up because I need you to listen," he says. "Focus. Think you can do that?"

"Please...wh...what do you want from me?"

"The truth," he says. "That's all."

He reaches for my left hand. Tied the way I am, I can't resist. "I don't want to hurt you if I don't have to," Derek says. "But you need to know that I'm serious. If I think you're lying..." With his other hand, he pulls out what he had shoved into his pants pocket and shows it to me.

A pair of garden shears. Curved. Sharp.

Slowly, even gently, he opens them and slides the little finger of my left hand in between the razor edges.

"One finger for each lie," he says. "Do you understand?"

Oh God! Oh Jesus! All at once, I'm sweating, my eyes stinging.

"Do you understand?" he asks again, voice unchanging, low key.

"Yes," I croak. My eyes remain riveted to the shears, expecting them to move, to squeeze.

"Chris. Look at me."

I look up into those dead eyes.

"I meant what I said." He stops to cough again, continues. "I need to understand everything. This," he says, indicating the blades lightly caressing my finger, "will help you to tell the truth. That's all I want. Don't tell me what you think I want to hear. There's no right or wrong answer. There's only the truth. Do you understand?"

But I can't tell him the truth. Not the whole truth.

My eyes dart back to the shears.

Abruptly, he squeezes them. "Do you *understand*?"

"Yes!" I cry out, eyes shooting back to him. "Please don't—"

"Shhh…"

He eases the pressure, and I let out a long, shaky breath. "Don't hold anything back," he says. "I want to hear all of it."

"I don't know what else I can tell you about that night…other than what I told the police."

"Start with that."

I look at him, confused. "What?"

"Tell me how your conversation with the police went."

I stare at him. I can hear the fear in my voice as I ask, "Are you going to kill me?"

"Why?" he comes back with. "Do you think you deserve to die?"

How long was I in this room before I woke up? Has Mom reported me missing? Are the police looking for me at this very moment?

If I can somehow stall, is there a chance they'll find me? Could they come bursting into this room any minute?

I stare into his lifeless eyes, looking for…I don't know… something that tells me I have a chance to survive this.

His eyes tell me nothing.

"If I cooperate," I say after a deep breath, "if I tell you what you want to know, will you let me go?"

"What I want to know is simply the truth. Now get started."

But I can't tell him the truth. Not all of it. Not the one, most important thing. I won't. Even if he cuts off every finger I have, telling him the truth would make him do far worse. But maybe I can tell him just enough. Enough to get me through this.

I swallow, wishing I had more water.

Giving the garden shears a slight squeeze for emphasis, Derek says, "Remember. Don't leave anything out."

"Once we got to the station," I begin, trying to keep the trembling out of my voice, but failing, "the police put me in an interrogation room…"

2

THEN

"It was just you and Devon in the house, right?" the detective says.

"Right," I hear myself respond.

He waves his hand for me to talk.

———

After Devon and I play two games of dice baseball, we order pizza and watch the Phillies game on TV—Devon making up trivia questions between innings from the huge baseball stats book I gave him that's sitting in his lap. I send him off to bed. He wants to keep talking baseball, but I point out he's not the only one who has school tomorrow.

I go to bed about eleven thirty. Fall into what I hope is a sound sleep.

But the same bad dream wakes me up again.

I lunge for Dad's gun on the floor…

I sit up in a cold sweat. Why the dream is back after three years is not something I'm going to figure out now, so I try closing my eyes again.

Then I hear something.

"That was around one o'clock?" the detective asks.

"I…I think so," I answer. "Yeah."

His name's Bob Fyfe. He says he knew my dad when they were both patrolmen, so maybe I remember him. I don't, but I made like I did.

The room is too cold. I can't stop shaking.

He puts a hand on my arm. "It's gonna be all right, Chris. I promise. Why don't you drink some of that Coke?"

I hate Coke, but he bought it for me and I don't want to piss him off by asking for something else. The carbonation burns going down.

"Go on," he says after I put the can back on the table.

"Where's Devon?" I ask.

"He's okay. You'll be able to see him soon. We got through to your mom too. She's on her way."

He looks at the notes in his hand from when we first talked at my house.

The image of blood on the kitchen counter flashes in my mind.

"I know it's difficult, but it's important we go through this again."

"I'm okay," I lie.

I'm not sure he believes me, but he goes on. "You said something woke you?"

"Yeah."

"How'd you know it wasn't your mom?"

"I know the noises she makes coming home late after a night shift at the diner; this wasn't like that."

"You checked on your brother?"

"Yes. I thought he'd be asleep."

I can see him the way he was lying on his side facing away from me, tangled up in his Phillies blanket. Normally, I'd have taken the time to straighten the blanket out, get him back into a more comfortable position. He was wearing a Ryan Howard T-shirt and gym shorts for pajamas. The walls of his room are covered with

thumbtacked baseball posters and baseball cards. Signed
baseballs from Phillies events, along with game balls and
home run balls he's collected from Little League games
he's played, decorate his shelves.

"But he wasn't."

"No. He rolled over to look at me and asked what
was going on. I told him to go back to sleep."

"But then you heard more noise. That's why you
went downstairs."

"Yes. Well…I'm not sure. I thought I did."

"Did Devon hear it?"

"I don't know. I just told him to stay in his room."

"Then you went and got the gun."

I hesitate. Look down at the table.

Detective Fyfe leans in. "These are the kinds of questions you're going to be asked in a little while, Chris. It's
better if you hear them from me first."

I take in another breath. Let it out.

"So you went and got the gun?" Detective Fyfe
says again.

I nod. "I was thinking, what would my dad do in this
situation," I tell him. "And I knew, if he thought one
of us might be in danger, he'd take along protection."

"And you thought Devon might be in danger. He was
awake. Worried. That's why you got your father's gun."

"Mom put his gun away a long time ago. But she has this smaller one Dad got her. For protection. After he died, Mom started keeping it loaded in a drawer next to her bed. She told me about it a couple years ago, told me where the key was if ever…" I stop, get my breath again.

"You went downstairs…" Detective Fyfe prompts.

"I didn't think I'd find anything. I really didn't. I thought I was being stupid. But then I got to the bottom of the stairs…"

To the left is the living room. I see the game board pieces and dice still spread out on the coffee table. I told Devon I'd put the game away, but I was so tired after he finally settled in, I forgot about it. Mom doesn't need to find this when she comes home.

I've almost finished cleaning it up when I hear something again. From the kitchen. A cabinet door being closed, another one being opened.

I stand up and start walking in that direction.

"He didn't see me at first," I say. "He was rooting around in a cabinet, his back to me. It was dark. Then I heard movement behind me from the living room—Devon. He must have come down the stairs. He called out my name, and the guy must have heard him 'cause he turned real quick, and there was something in his right hand. It looked like…"

"What?" Detective Fyfe says. "What did it look like?"

"It was dark, hard to see… I thought he was pointing it at me…"

The detective waits.

"And my gun went off. Just like that."

"You…pulled the trigger."

"I guess. I…I don't remember. It…it just happened."

"What do you mean?"

"I… It fired. That's all. It just fired. And he fell. It all happened so fast. I went right over to him. There was blood on the counter. Blood on the floor. It was pumping out of him."

"Where was Devon?"

"Like I said, in the living room. I shouted for him to stay there. He did. Then I went right to the guy on the floor."

"Is it possible Devon saw what happened?"

"No. He never came into the kitchen."

"We'll be talking to him." I look at Detective Fyfe. "We have to, Chris." After a moment, he tells me, "Keep going."

I swallow. "I saw the guy was alive, and I called 911. Then I went back to him, and this time, he wasn't moving. I thought he must be dead. That's when I noticed...how young he looked."

"Then what happened?"

"I started looking for..."

"What?"

"His gun. I...I didn't see it..."

Abruptly, Detective Fyfe gets up and moves away from the table. He seems to be thinking.

Now he's going to arrest me. He has no choice.

After a moment, he says in a low voice, his back still to me, "You thought he had a gun."

"I... He was pointing something—"

"That you thought was a gun," he says in a more measured tone.

"I don't know—"

"No!" His voice makes me jump.

I stare at him as he turns and moves slowly back toward me. "Don't say that, okay?" he says quietly. "There *was* a gun."

"There was?" I say, anxious.

"Yes." He lets his hands fall on the table, leans in toward me. He's a big, burly guy. Big hands. Fierce eyes. I wonder how many suspects he's intimidated in here.

"You're a lucky kid, you know that?" he says. "If you'd reacted just a little slower, taken just a couple seconds longer to pull the trigger, it might have been you on the floor instead of the other guy. You did the right thing. You protected yourself. You protected your brother."

"My brother?"

"If he'd shot you first, he might have gone after Devon. Who knows?"

My heart is pounding hard against my chest. He says there was a gun, so there must have been.

But I can feel myself walking over, the body coming into view as I reach the other side of the counter. Again, I see the blood on the counter near where he went down. The bullet got him in the neck. The blood kept coming. The guy—not just a guy, a kid, younger than me—was looking at me, shaking, his eyes pleading, like he wanted to tell me something but couldn't.

"We found the gun under his body," Detective Fyfe says. "He must have fallen on it. So you wouldn't have seen it after he was down." Moving his chair closer to me, he sits again and puts a hand on my shoulder. "It's gonna be okay, Chris. Your father is still loved around here. What he did three years ago..." He hesitates, then says, "We owe him. So we're gonna watch out for you. We're gonna make sure this doesn't turn into something it isn't. But it's important what you say to the assistant DA when she's here. And how you say it. You need to be consistent. She's gonna ask why you chose to go downstairs with a gun rather than call the police right away, especially since there was a phone right in your mom's room. But you said it yourself. You weren't sure; it could have been nothing. You took the gun because that was what your father would have wanted you to do. Watch out for your ten-year-old brother. You're only sixteen yourself. Not too many adults would be brave enough to do what you did.

"Once you were in the kitchen, you hardly had time to react. There he was, pointing a gun at you, and you fired; you *had* to fire. Self-defense, plain and simple." Detective Fyfe leans in, lowers his voice. "But you don't have to make a big deal about not seeing the gun for sure. It was there; we found it. All you have to say is, he turned, pointed his gun, so you shot him. You saw how bad he was hurt and called 911 right away. Okay?"

I take a deep, shuddery breath and nod. He pats me on the shoulder. "You're gonna be okay."

He moves away like he might leave but stops, turns

back, and stares at me a moment. "You don't really remember me, do you?" he says.

I hesitate. "No. I...I'm sorry."

"That's all right. I was already a detective when your dad died. I tried to get him to take the detective's exam after me, told him he'd ace it. But he wanted to stay in uniform. Said he loved it. When we were both patrolmen, I remember you running around your backyard at the barbecues he'd throw. You were four, five years old.

"After the funeral, I spoke to you at your house, shook your hand, but I'm sure you had too much to deal with." He hesitates, sighs. "He was a great guy, your dad. What he did... He's a hero. A lot of us still miss him."

Suddenly, I remember this guy. Can see him standing tall in front of me, hand extended, one of the many firm, solemn handshakes I'd gotten the day of Dad's funeral. Just another cop telling me how sorry he was.

Except that, when Mom left for a moment to take Devon to the bathroom—Devon had been very needy that day and refused to let Mom out of his sight—he leaned down close to me and said in a quiet, tense voice no one else could hear, "Don't worry, son. The punk who did this is gonna pay." Then he had straightened, tousled my hair, smiled, and said, "Don't let your mom down. You're the man of the house now."

"I'm gonna see if your mom's here," he says now, back at the table. "And I'll get Devon and bring him in. You can have a few minutes till the ADA arrives. Your mom can stay during the questioning but not your brother. He'll be questioned on his own, after you. But your mom can be with him as well."

"Who was he?" I ask. "The…the kid…"

Detective Fyfe looks at me. "The intruder you mean. Don't worry about that right now."

"I…I'm just…"

"Don't worry about it." One more time he puts a hand on my shoulder. "Remember what we talked about. Keep it succinct, consistent."

I nod, and he smiles, and for a moment I think he's going to tousle my hair like he did three years ago.

But, instead, he turns and walks out of the room. Leaving me alone. Still shaking. Then Devon bursts into the room and hugs me, and for a few minutes anyway, things are better.

3

"So this Detective Fyfe shaped your story for you," Derek says.

"What do you mean?" I ask.

"He told you what to tell the assistant DA."

"He...was just trying to be helpful."

"Helpful." Derek shakes his head. "That's what you call it? Asking you to lie?"

"I didn't lie."

"Oh, really?" His grip tightens on the garden shears.

"Please, don't..."

"Did you see the gun in his hand?"

Sweat from my forehead stings my eyes, and I try to blink the pain away. "He turned, he pointed it at me, and I...I just reacted... My gun went off."

"But did you *see* the *gun*?"

"He...had it. He might have shot me, so I shot him. It was self-defense. After I shot him, he fell on the gun. That's why I didn't see it afterward. The police found it. Detective Fyfe told me."

"And Detective Fyfe wouldn't lie, right?" he says in a harsh growl.

"No."

"The only way you'd know for sure is if you can say you saw the gun in my brother's hand."

"The police—"

All of a sudden, he is on his feet, with both hands now around the handle of the garden shears. "Do you think I'm kidding?" he spits, his voice now a harsh growl. "Do you think I won't cut off this finger?"

"No! I believe you! Please—"

"*Did you see the gun in his hand?*"

"*I don't know!*"

"What do you mean you don't—?"

"I want to be able to tell you. I do! It was so fast... and then my gun went off...and then he was falling... And when I think back to it, sometimes I see the gun and sometimes I don't. I can't be sure…but Detective Fyfe said they found the gun under his body, so he must've…"

"You think you're going to get by with a story like that?" he seethes. "You think you can just—"

"If I were lying, I wouldn't tell you I wasn't sure!" I shout. "I'd just tell you what Detective Fyfe told me to say!"

Hearing that, he hesitates. "Maybe," he says.

He's going to do it. I can tell. I can feel the sharp edge start to press, starting to cut.

"Or maybe you—"

All at once, he begins to cough again, and the pressure stops. It sounds much harsher than before, and he pulls away, the blades releasing their grip as his coughing fit continues for at least a full minute, his body bent at the waist and turned away from me as he fights to regain control. In that moment, I look down at my left hand, expecting to see my little finger hanging by only the flesh. But I'm shocked to see no blood. There's just a scratch from where his coughing spasm caused him to pull the garden shears back, scraping the skin.

Finally he stops, but instead of coming toward me, he simply stares.

Waiting to see what he might do next is almost as bad as when I thought he was going to cut my finger off.

After a minute, he simply says, "Go on."

I look back at him, confused. "What?"

"Keep talking."

"I told you. I can't remember—"

"I know, I know," he says, waving the hand holding the garden shears as he returns to the chair. "You can't remember if you saw a gun. Maybe that's true. I'll decide later."

After more seconds pass, I ask, "What more do you want me to say?"

"What happened after you finished talking to the police? Did you go home?"

"Yes."

"Go on from there."

"I don't understand."

He leans forward again, over the back of the chair. "Tell me what happened after you killed my brother. I want to know how it changed your life. How it changed *you*."

"Why would you want to know that?"

"The only thing you should care about is telling the truth." To emphasize this, he puts the garden shears back in place, once again embracing my little finger. "Now keep going."

I don't know what more this guy wants. I told him

what I told the detective. What more is there? Is there something *he* knows? Something he's not telling me? Is he waiting to see if I'll trip up, give him an excuse to cut me?

"You were finished with the cop, and you went home..." he urges.

All I know is I've still got all my fingers. I'm still alive. And people have got to be looking for me, don't they? If I keep stalling, maybe I can allow time for them to find me.

I take a shaky breath.

4

THEN

We don't leave the station till six thirty in the morning. The first few miles home, no one says anything. I glance in the rearview mirror. Devon has his head down. I can't see his face. Finally, Mom says that Devon and I are not going to school today and suggests the three of us stay in a hotel for the day instead of going home. Get some rest, maybe go somewhere fun. She can call in at the diner. We can go home tomorrow.

"I've got a game tonight," Devon says in a quiet voice.

"Well, I'm sure one game—"

"No way you're gonna miss your game, buddy," I assure him. I look at Mom. She frowns at me then glances away.

A few more miles of silence pass before Devon mumbles, "I don't want to go to a hotel."

"That's fine," Mom says after a moment. "We'll go home. But no school. We need sleep. You especially, Devon."

As it turns out, he can barely keep his eyes open as we pull in the driveway. I walk him into the house and right up to his room. "Don't forget to wake me in time for the game," he mumbles as he settles in, still wearing the clothes he'd changed into before going to the police station.

"You got it." I sit with him for a moment, rubbing his back as he closes his eyes. Not two minutes later, he begins to snore. Looking at the two of us, you might not think we were brothers. He's blond and I'm dark haired. And even though he's only ten, he seems broader and stronger than me, with my skinny frame. Another year or two at most and he'll be taller than I'll ever be.

I hear the phone ringing from the extension in Mom's room as I stand up. As I come out of Devon's room, Mom steps into the hallway, phone in hand. "It's for you," she says, handing it to me before heading downstairs.

It's Terry, calling from school. Terry lives a couple

houses down the street from us; we've been best friends since he moved into the neighborhood when we were eight. He has a younger brother as well. Brady and Devon play together on the same Little League team.

Because he's in band, Terry gets to school earlier than I do. I hear the sound of kids talking in the background, somebody blowing a trumpet. "Chris, are you all right?" he asks. "I saw the cop cars last night. I wanted to come over, but Mom wouldn't let me."

"I'm okay," I mumble.

"Kids are talking stupid here. Guys are saying you shot some dude. That's crazy, right?"

I hesitate, mumble something like, "Somebody broke in..."

"What? You mean it's true? Jesus, Chris..." A pause. "Are you coming in late today?"

"No. We just got back from the police station a little while ago. We need to sleep."

"Sure, that makes sense. What was I thinking? Jeez, the police station. How's Devon doing? What about the game tonight? Sorry, that's a stupid question."

"We'll be there."

"Really? Okay. Cool. Uh...I'll see you tonight. We'll talk then."

"Okay." Feeling a little dazed, I hang up.

Downstairs, I find Mom in the living room, drinking a glass of wine even though it's morning.

She sees me looking at the glass and shrugs self-consciously. "I'm going to sleep soon."

I consider getting myself a glass of orange juice but it means going into the kitchen, where you can still see faded blood on the counter. As if reading my mind, Mom says, "Tomorrow, I'm buying the best cleanser I can find and scrubbing down the whole kitchen. It's been needing it for a while anyway."

I join her on the sofa. "You call Devon's school?" I ask.

"Yeah. Your school too. And work."

The baseball dice game still sits open on the coffee table, the dice and board pieces still waiting to be put away. Mom has closed the front window curtains, but the two edges don't quite meet, so I can still see outside. The day looks dreary, but it's supposed to clear up by early afternoon.

Mom takes a couple more sips of wine then says without looking at me, "It's just a game, you know. I would imagine after what happened it wouldn't be a bad idea—"

"I think we should keep things as normal as possible for him," I tell her.

After a moment, she nods. "I guess that makes sense." She takes another sip, glances at me. "He told the police he didn't see anything. He heard the gunshot but that was it; he stayed in the living room. Is that true?"

"Yes. He stayed there until the police arrived."

"He never saw the body? At any time."

"No."

"Thank God." She takes another sip of wine.

We sit in silence.

"I'm sorry I wasn't here," she says, frowning. "I should have been home a lot sooner."

"It's okay. I knew you'd be late."

"I shouldn't have been that late."

She goes back to her wine but after a moment puts it down and says, "I need to ask you, and you need to tell me the truth: What you told the assistant DA, that's what really happened?"

My heart wants to jump up into my throat, and I swallow hard. "What...what do you mean?"

"I know what those guys at the station would do to protect you because of your father, what he still means to them..." She pauses a moment. "I know Bob Fyfe probably helped you shape your story for the ADA. I just want you to know...if it didn't happen exactly the way you told it, it's okay. If...I don't know...they had to do something at the scene—"

"Like what?"

She looks at me.

"The guy had a gun. He pointed it at me. I fired. I didn't want to, but I did. End of story."

She continues to stare at me. Mom's not one to just let things go. I wait for her to push. But, surprisingly, she just nods. Leans in. "Then you did the right thing."

She seems about to put her arm around me but picks up her wineglass and empties it instead. Mom's never been one for hugs or kissing boo-boos, even when Devon and I were little. She's grown even tougher since Dad was killed.

"I'm going to bed," she says. "You should too." Leaving her glass on the coffee table, she stands.

"I'll set an alarm," I tell her. She looks at me. "So we're up in time for Devon's game."

"Right." She gives me a half smile. "Always looking out for us, aren't you? I don't know what I'd do without you." She leans forward "You did good, Chris. You did real good."

She seems a little off balance as she heads up the stairs. How much wine did she have before I sat down? I realize I never asked her how her date went. She'd only started dating again in the last few months. The first two tries didn't go beyond the first date, but this guy was different, she'd said.

I set the alarm on my cell and have every intention of going upstairs to my room and bed as well. But I start drifting and tell myself I'll stretch out here on the couch for just a few minutes.

———

"Shoot him! Shoot him!" I'm screaming at Dad. But Dad's moving toward the girl instead, so I lunge for Dad's gun on the floor because if I can get to it before the guy fires—

I wake up and stop short of crying out. Mom is leaning over me, her hand on my shoulder. I realize I never made it off the sofa.

"You okay?" she says, eyes wide.

"Yeah, I... Sorry, I..." I sit up. Through the crack between the curtains I can tell that the sun has pushed aside the day's grayness, just as the weather report promised.

"Didn't mean to scare you," she says, excitement in her voice. "That was Bob Fyfe on the phone." I hadn't even heard it ringing. "Good news. They're calling it a clear case of self-defense. The case is closed. It's over."

"Over?" I mumble, picking at some crust in my eye.

"Well, the ADA had a little trouble with the fact you went and got the gun instead of just calling the police. But the gun's registered, right?" She hesitates then adds,

"Turns out there've been a few incidents in the neighborhood, people reporting that when they got up in the morning they could tell someone had been in the house and gone through their stuff. One report had a couple waking up and seeing someone running out their front door. You're the one who just happened to catch him."

She nods her head. "But it's over. You have nothing to worry about." Her eyes go to the sofa. "Why don't you go up?"

"What time is it?" I ask.

"Noon. You can sleep for a few more hours. I think I'm going to. Later, I'll order in something for us, a late lunch, early dinner, whatever." When I don't move, she adds, "Come on. Your bed's gotta be better than this sofa."

"What was his name?" I ask suddenly.

"Who?"

"The...intruder. Did Detective Fyfe tell you?"

"I don't know and I don't care." She looks scared.

I look away. Maybe I should say something, but I don't know what.

"The important thing is, you're safe. You and Devon both. Go to bed," she says.

After a moment, I nod. Following Mom up, I watch her go into her room before I walk into mine.

It's harder to fall asleep this time. When I close my

eyes, I see a figure turning toward me, pointing something. It's hidden in shadow.

Gunfire.

The image repeats itself several times before it finally stops. After a while, I'm finally able to fall asleep.

At least this time, the dream leaves me alone.

5

THEN

We get to the ball field forty-five minutes early, as Coach Neville requires. As always, he greets each one of his players as they arrive. He normally gives Devon, his best hitter, an extra big welcome, but this time he seems cautious. I'm sure word's gotten around.

After Devon has joined the other boys, the coach walks up to Mom and me. A look of concern knots up his wide features. "I heard what happened," he says. "Is he okay? Do you think I should—?"

"He's fine," I say before Mom can respond. "Just let him play as he normally would. It's better that way."

The coach nods. "Normal. Yeah, I get that." He looks at me. "Are *you* okay?"

"I'm fine," I tell him.

He nods again, then reaches out and gives me a firm handshake. "Damn brave of you, son. I don't know if I'd be able to do it." He squeezes my shoulder. "Damn brave." Finally, he turns and walks over to the team. Mom and I head for the minor league field bleachers.

Next year, after he has turned eleven, Devon will move up to Maple Braden Little League's "major league" level. This year, at five foot four, he's already taller than all the other kids playing at the "minor league" level. He's had a monster season. I think the other teams have stopped trying to figure out how to pitch to him and just hope that when he hits the inevitable home run, it doesn't happen at too crucial a moment in the game.

Dad used to say, "Devon believes you're as happy to see him as he is to see you," and he was right. He's friendly with everyone. Everyone likes Devon. He was the kind of little kid who'd walk up to people he didn't know and say hi. Mom and Dad took special care in explaining the rules to him about talking to strangers.

Devon was seven when our father was killed. When Mom told him, I was right there, trying my best to keep the tears back and stay brave for him. The look of utter heartbreak on his face as he cried in my mother's arms broke my heart. If I'd had any doubts before, from that moment on, I knew it was my job to be there for him. No matter what.

It's what my dad would want.

Normally, after Mom and I have found our places on the bleachers, Terry comes over. But this time I see him talking with Matt, Ben, and Eric. I'm surprised to see them; they never hang out at the Little League ball fields during games—most of the kids from school don't unless they have a brother involved, and even those that do, I don't see them here every game like Terry and I are.

Terry waves for me to come over.

"You want something from the snack bar?" I ask Mom.

"No." She doesn't look at me. I think she still believes Devon should have stayed home from the game after what happened last night, even if winning this game does give the team a bye in the playoffs, which means time to rest pitching arms. As I approach Terry, Matt, fair haired and wearing the usual tight T-shirt to show off his muscles, steps forward and says, "So this is where you two doofuses hang out during the spring." He gives me one of his smiles. "I hear your brother's a big home-run hitter, Chris."

"What are you doing here?" I ask.

"You weren't at school today," he says. "Terry said you were gonna be here. We wanted to talk to you about what happened."

I look at Terry. He shrugs and says, "They wanted to know what I knew. I told them it was better if they talked to you themselves."

"Hey, you're famous now." Ben gives me a light punch.

"Yeah, right," I scoff, feeling my face begin to burn.

"I already heard they cleared you. Called it self-defense. That is cool."

"Cool?"

"How you stood up like that," Ben says.

"You're gonna tell us all about it, right?" Eric asks.

"Tell…?"

"You're not gonna leave us out of the loop, are you?" Matt says. "We want to hear all about it." He points his finger like it's a gun and makes a popping sound.

"I…I can't now. Devon's got a game…"

"Well, I figure we could talk some during the game—"

"It's an important game," I say, sounding lame. "For the playoffs. I should watch."

Matt looks irritated but then his face bursts into a grin. "Sure," he says, "we understand. Your brother—what's his name?"

"Devon."

"Right. It's cool the way you are with him. Especially after your dad died. He must think you're a hero now."

When I don't respond, Matt asks, "You doing anything this weekend?"

"Don't...don't know."

"Maybe we can take you out. Then you can tell us all about it."

"I...I don't think—"

"He's probably got reporters hounding him, big story like that," Ben says. "You could end up on Fox News talking to Sean Hannity."

"All right," Matt says. "Monday at school. Lunchtime." He's still smiling, but I can tell he's not happy about having to wait. "But we want details." He leans in. "I'd stay, watch your brother play, but I got a date." He winks. "I hope he hits a home run."

Pointing at me again like his finger's a gun, he makes another popping sound then walks away. The others follow him out of the complex.

Terry clears his throat and says, "You going to the snack bar?"

On the way, it seems like everybody we pass is looking at me. Some nod their heads. A few look away.

Terry orders a hot dog. I just get a bottle of water, but when I try to give a dollar to Mrs. Wheat, who runs the snack bar, she pushes it back into my hand. "It's on the house, Chris," she says. "From now on, it's always on the house."

She turns to another customer. I look at Terry, shrug, and put the dollar back in my pocket.

On the way back, Jon Roney, a father whose son is also on the team, stops me. "I want to shake your hand," he says. His grip is too hard, and I try not to wince. "I want you to know—a lot of us want you to know—we're behind you one hundred percent. There are going to be some who'll try to turn this into something else. Don't let them get to you. Guy like that, breaking and entering, who knows what might have happened if you hadn't... You stood up for your family. Hell, you stood up for the whole neighborhood. That was a brave thing you did, son."

He squeezes my shoulder, then nods and goes back to the bleachers. The people he is sitting with smile in my direction. I don't know what to do, so I smile back.

Is it possible word hasn't gotten around yet that it wasn't just a *guy*, it was a *kid*? Maybe the police are keeping that part quiet. For now.

Terry and I find a place on the bleachers away from other people for the moment. He unwraps his hot dog, takes a bite, and looks out at the field. I look at my bottle of water and decide I'm not thirsty.

We watch the coach hit balls to the team. I catch Terry glancing sideways at me a couple of times. His brother, playing shortstop, makes a nice play on a pop-up, pedaling backward into shallow left field. "Nice catch, Brady!" Terry shouts.

Unlike Devon and me, no one would doubt Terry and Brady are brothers. Like me, Terry is no athlete, but he still shares his brother's reddish-brown hair and wide-eyed demeanor.

Taking a couple more bites, Terry looks at me. "You think Devon's gonna hit another one out tonight?"

"Maybe," I say. Devon's on a tear. He's hit seven homers in his last five games.

Silence again. Terry finishes his hot dog. I'm thinking I should say something when Terry says, "Hey, are you mad at me?"

I look at him. "About what?"

"Telling those guys you were gonna be here."

I just shrug. I'm not sure how I feel about it, actually.

"They were asking me questions at school, wondered

if I knew anything, and I just told them you'd be here tonight, that they could ask you—"

"It's all right," I tell him. "No big deal."

Terry looks at me. "You doing okay?" he asks.

Again, I shrug. "Yeah."

"I was surprised you were coming tonight."

"It's important to Devon," I say. "He *needs* to be here."

"Everybody's talking about it," Terry says. "From what I hear, most people think you did the right thing."

"*Most* people, huh?"

"My dad says you're a hero. Like your father was. A lot of people are saying that."

The two teams have finished going through their drills. I see Devon trotting toward his team's dugout, a focused look in his eyes, getting his game face on.

"So you're really okay?"

"I don't think it's sunk in yet," I mutter.

"What do you mean?"

"It still feels like it could have been a bad dream. I'm gonna wake up any minute and things will be back to normal." It's the same way I felt when Mom told me Dad had been killed and that she was going to need me to be strong for Devon, because he was only seven and it was going to be especially hard on him.

We watch the head coach from each team meeting

with the umpire, talking over the ground rules. The other team's coach seems a little intense. His team's tied with ours for second place, so he needs a win to get a bye, like we do. Whoever loses will have to play in the first round.

"What's it like?" Terry asks.

"What?" I say.

I'm glad the sudden cheer as Devon's team takes the field cuts off Terry's response before I get the chance to learn what he meant. I watch Devon take his position at first base. His team's the White Sox.

"I'm gonna go sit with Mom," I tell Terry.

"Sure. You know my parents; they'll want me sitting with them to start. I'll come over third or fourth inning."

I walk back to my seat. Mom smiles at me. "Devon seems okay," she says. "Maybe you were right. This is good, him playing."

Devon bats cleanup, and when he first comes up, it's the bottom of the first inning. His team has runners on first and second with one out and the other team, the Mariners, is already ahead, 2–0. As a result of Devon's recent spurt of home runs, a group of kids stand on the other side of the outfield fence, shouting for him to hit one out so they can catch it.

Devon hits a ground ball to the second baseman

instead, who throws him out at first, moving up the runners. But thanks to a wild pitch on the next batter, Brady, who's on third, comes dashing in. I hear Terry and his parents' cheering above all the others.

His next time up, Devon obliges the chanting kids, launching one of his laser shots high over everyone's head to the T-ball field beyond where, fortunately, no one is playing. After three innings, the White Sox are in the lead for the first time.

Devon gets another hit, a single, in the fifth. But by the time his team comes up for the bottom of the sixth, the last inning, things have gone bad, and the White Sox are facing a six-run deficit.

"This doesn't look good," I hear Mom mutter under her breath. But she claps her hands and shouts encouragement with the rest of the White Sox fans.

Terry had joined me at the top of the fourth. I hear him repeating, "We can do this, we can do this." He looks at me. "If they can get a rally going and get to Devon, he could win it with a home run."

It would take a big rally to get to Devon's spot in the order.

But the boys put together a string of hits, and when Devon comes up, they are trailing by only a run with one out and no one on base. A home run will tie the game.

Everyone's buzzing. The kids are chanting beyond the outfield fence. Devon gets two strikes on him before he hits one long enough to clear the fence, but it's foul. You can hear everyone letting out a collective breath as the pitcher sets himself to throw the next pitch. Devon hits the ball hard. It doesn't clear the fence but he gets a double. So now he's in scoring position, representing the tying run with one out. The next batter walks. Now the tying *and* winning runs are on. The Mariners' coach brings in a new pitcher, the third of the inning. Our next batter comes to the plate. People are cheering, shouting.

He strikes out.

Now there are two outs. The noise of the crowd rises up again as the kid who could be our final batter steps up. I watch Devon lean toward third. He's not allowed to leave the bag until the ball crosses home plate, but he wants to get a good jump.

The batter swings and misses the first pitch. Then he works the count to two and two. The runners get ready. Coach Neville, handling third base, shouts to Devon, "Run on anything!" Devon has an intense look on his face.

The batter swings and hits a ground ball just past the second baseman's reach. A single. The right fielder is there to grab it. Devon's not going to be able to score. But we're still alive. Second place and a bye is still within reach. His coach is telling him to hold up at third. The bases are going to be loaded.

But to everyone's surprise, Devon runs through the coach's stop sign, chugging toward home plate. As big as he is, Devon must look to the catcher like a tank approaching. The right fielder is caught by surprise but recovers quickly and guns the throw. Devon still has a quarter of the way to go when the catcher catches the ball and turns.

Since the catcher has the ball in hand, the runner must slide to try and score. This is so the catcher or runner doesn't get hurt from a collision at the plate.

Devon's not fast, but he's smart and an excellent slider. If he slides to the back part of the plate, maybe he can elude the tag.

But he doesn't slide. Instead, his head goes down and his arms come up like a football tackle about to block, and he slams into the catcher, knocking him onto his back. The ball rolls away.

The impulse is to cheer. Score tied. But the umpire points to Devon and roars, "Illegal collision! *You're out!*" He emphasizes it with a pump of his fist.

Both players are down, but Devon, after a moment,

gets up. The catcher stays on the ground a while longer, but eventually, he's on his feet too.

Mom starts to stand, but I grab her arm. "Don't."

"But he might be hurt."

"You'll only embarrass him. Just wait. He's fine."

Our coach is arguing with the umpire but to no avail. It's clear what happened. Running into the catcher is illegal, and as a result, he's out. Game over. White Sox lose.

"Why...why did he do that?" I hear Terry say next to me. "The coach had him held up."

I don't answer. All around me, I hear people talking to each other.

"What was he doing? Didn't he see the stop sign?"

"Kid that size, he might have really hurt him."

"Surely not on purpose. Not a nice boy like Devon."

"What's the family doing here, anyway? Would you feel like playing a baseball game if your brother had just killed somebody in your own house?"

"Shhhh, Jack. They're right over there."

I watch Devon as he is led back to the dugout bench and made to sit down. He seems fine physically, better than the catcher, who is limping away, his coach barking in anger at the umpire and pointing at Devon.

Mom can't wait any longer and goes down to see him. As I watch her head toward the dugout where Coach

Neville is talking to Devon, his arm around his shoulders, the look I saw on his face as he headed toward home plate pops into my head.

It's the second time I've seen him look like that.

"I gotta go. Talk to you later," Terry says before he walks away and heads toward Brady.

I watch Mom finally reach Devon, and I wait while she talks to him.

6

NOW

"What," Derek cuts in, "your kid brother never made a mistake before? Big star baseball player gets called out and doesn't get to be the hero this time, so boo-de-boo-hoo?"

I don't say anything. I don't know what to say.

"He's so good, he's perfect, I guess."

"He's a better ballplayer than that," I tell him, feeling defensive.

"I see. He gets thrown out at home plate, your mom makes him go to bed without his supper?"

"No. It's not—"

"What? It's not what, for Chrissake?"

"Look, you told me not to leave out anything."

Derek stares at me for a moment. "True," he says finally, the garden shears not moving. "Okay then. You were saying, 'It's not…'?"

I take a breath. "It's not like him to knock the catcher down like that. Or to ignore what the coach told him to do. It's…"

"Mean," Derek responds after a moment. "Christ, he's a ten-year-old kid. All ten-year-olds are mean."

"No, you don't understand." The look on Derek's face makes me stop. A look that says maybe I'm pushing things too far.

But after a long moment, he pulls back, letting out a sigh. "Maybe I don't understand. Explain it to me." With one hand, he gestures magnanimously, emphasizing that I continue.

With the other hand, he still holds the garden shears in place.

7

THEN

Devon goes up to his room as soon as we enter the house, and Mom follows. I wait downstairs. Two minutes later, Mom comes back, exasperated. "He won't say a word to me," she grumbles. "You go talk to him. He talks more to you than to me anyway."

Before I head up the stairs, I see Mom rooting in a drawer and pulling out a cigarette. I haven't seen her smoke in months. She sits and stares at it, struggling over whether or not to light it.

I find Devon lying on his bed. Seeing him like this reminds me he's going to need a new bed soon, as tall as he's getting. He still has his uniform on, including his muddy cleats, which he has up on the sheets.

"Get your cleats off," I tell him. When he doesn't comply, I raise my voice a little. "Devon…"

He uses each foot to shove the cleat off the other. They fall haphazardly on the floor, and he turns on his side away from me.

This isn't like him. "What's going on?" I ask, sitting next to him on the bed.

His face remains in a scowl. I can see he's been crying.

"Are you upset because of the game?" I'm almost positive that's not it.

He doesn't answer.

"It just means you get to play an extra game. Heck, that's no problem. I know you guys'll do well." Trying to keep things light.

Still nothing.

"Is it because you made the last out?"

After a few seconds, he shakes his head.

Part of me says to leave him alone for a while, that he'll tell me when he's ready.

But then I remember the look on his face as he came barreling in from third, and it scares me.

"You ignored the coach on purpose, didn't you?" I

ask. "You saw him put up the stop sign at third, but you went through it anyway."

Devon shifts his position but doesn't speak.

"You could have slid, but you put your arms up," I push. "Did the catcher do something or say something to you when you were batting that made you mad?"

Silence.

"Devon?"

Nothing.

In a quieter voice, I say, "It's not like you. Talk to me. Did you want to hurt him?"

Devon mumbles something.

"What? I didn't hear you."

"I'm sorry," Devon utters. He's fighting back more tears.

"He's going to be okay. Nothing serious."

"I lost the game for us."

"No, you didn't. And it was just one game, Devon. No big deal. Do your best. Have fun. If you win, great. If you don't, it's okay. You know that."

He nods.

"So if you're mad at yourself, don't—"

"I'm mad at *you*!"

His intensity shocks me. "At me? Why?"

"You shouldn't have—" He cuts himself off by shoving his face into his pillow.

I try to wait him out, but when it doesn't look like he's going to pull his face away anytime soon, I try, "Devon?"

He doesn't answer. Stays where he is.

"Devon!" I say more firmly. "Look at me."

After a few seconds, he lifts his head. His face is streaked with tears again. He still looks angry.

My mouth feels dry as I speak. "Why are you mad at me? It's okay to tell me."

Again, he says nothing.

"Devon?"

Silence.

"We've always been able to talk about stuff."

"I'm tired," he insists, defiance on his face.

"All right. Maybe later. You know you can talk to me about anything. Right?"

He wipes his nose with his hand.

"You need a shower before bed."

"Okay."

"Put your uniform in the hamper."

"I *know* that," he emphasizes. But sometimes, if I don't tell him, Mom or I will find it all bunched up on the floor near his bed.

"I think I better change those sheets. You got 'em dirty."

"I'll do it," he says, surprising me.

"That's all right. You get in the shower."

"*I'll* do it." He looks at me, scowling.

I don't push this time. "Okay."

I watch him as he yanks the sheets off the bed and throws them onto the floor.

He doesn't look at me.

———

I find Mom in her room. I knew she was in there, listening to us. I could smell the cigarette smoke.

"He's just being ornery," she says.

"It's not like him."

"Oh, come on. He's ten years old."

After a moment, I just shrug.

"Just talk to him later."

"I guess." I look at her. "Would you mind if I went for a walk?"

"No. Go ahead," Mom says. "Take your time. I'll get him to bed if you're not back."

Better she do it than me anyway, as angry as he seems to be with me.

8

THEN

It's still muggy outside. The hot summer weather came early; we don't usually get this till August.

I don't know why I'm out here. I don't go for walks anymore. I used to go for walks with Dad. Something we started when I was eight. We'd do it after dinner, just to talk about stuff. If he were on night shift, we'd walk together to the station, which is just six blocks from our house. One of his fellow cops coming off shift would take me home.

The last time I walked with him was the night before he was killed. He was going on day shift the next day, and he'd had two days off to get himself acclimated again from a month of nights. But he had agreed to pull a double shift to help someone out and was working that night straight through to the end of the next day. I was a little nervous about it because I always felt better when he was on the day shift. My thinking back then was that night shift was more dangerous because more bad people were out at night.

What did I know? Police can get killed during the day too.

After Dad died, I worked hard at remembering everything about our last walk, everything we talked about.

There was nothing special about that night. It was late summer; school was starting in about a week. Eighth grade. As is inevitable, Dad mentioned the Phillies. "Things didn't work out for them this year," he says, "but if they could just make the right move or two this off-season, they could be right back in the hunt, I'm telling you. Don't you think, Chris?"

"It'd be nice," I offered. By the time I was thirteen, I'd pretty much given up pretending I liked sports of any kind. It still didn't stop him from trying to talk about baseball with me, his true sports love, or from hoping that I would change someday and begin sharing that same love with him.

Not that it had really mattered at that point. He had Devon. And Devon absolutely loved baseball. He'd play it every day year-round if he could.

Dad would tell us how, when Devon and I each were babies, he would hold us in his favorite chair and read baseball box scores from the newspaper out loud every morning.

With Devon, it stuck.

Devon has natural instincts when it comes to athletics. He has Dad's blond hair and fair complexion, and is big and strong through the chest and shoulders, like our father was. I have Mom's dark coloring, angular face, and I'm slender, like she is. And I have no athletic ability whatsoever. Comparing the way the two of us move, Devon has a smoothness and grace I've never had, even as big as he is. Me, I'm just gawky.

"I'm glad they're starting that fall league and Devon's going to get a chance to play baseball some more," Dad said. "You wait and see. Your brother's hitting is going to get a lot better. His bat's slow right now because he's so big for his age and he's still getting used to his own body. But one day, maybe in fall ball, maybe next summer, the light's gonna go on, and then, watch out. When he starts getting hits, they're gonna be monsters."

Dad never got to see the results of that light going on in his younger son's mind, or know the success Devon is having now, the reputation he's gained.

I know he'd be proud.

I don't know why I decided to walk this way; it's too painful, even after three years.

Time to go back. I'm standing in front of the police station as I turn back the way I came.

"Chris." Detective Fyfe is coming out of the station. "Do you need something?"

I remember more about him now. Throwing a baseball with me at those barbecues when I was seven, eight years old. Giving me pointers. Not that they did much good.

Again, I remember him talking to me at Dad's funeral.

Don't worry, Chris. The punk who did this is gonna pay.

"What are you doing here?" he asks.

I shrug. "Just walking."

"Do you want a ride back home?"

"It's only six blocks."

"Okay. I'll see you around then."

I don't even realize I'm going to ask the question until he starts to walk away and I blurt out, "Can you tell me who he was?"

Detective Fyfe stops, looks back at me. "Who?"

"The kid I...shot." I let out a long breath. "What was his name?"

He stares at me a moment.

Finally he says, "Come with me."

There's a bench half a block from the station next to the Maple-Braden war memorial honoring the township's residents who have died in war. We sit.

"You haven't watched the local news reports about this on TV?"

I shake my head.

"Why are you asking then?" Detective Fyfe says.

"I don't know. He must have a family. Maybe I should...talk to them, try to explain—"

"You *definitely* should *not* do that. Got it?"

After a moment, I nod, and Detective Fyfe looks away. He stares straight ahead for a moment before looking at me again. "I'm only telling you this now because there's gonna be an article about it in the paper tomorrow. You'd eventually find out on your own anyway. His name was Caleb Brannick."

"Was he from around here?" I ask.

"He lived a couple of townships over. We're pretty sure he did those other break-ins around here too."

"He was in school?"

"No. He'd been on his own for about four months after he ran away from home."

"How old was he?"

"Thirteen."

"Jesus." After a long moment, I whisper, "That's not...that's not even high school."

"He was in seventh grade. Though, like I said, he was a runaway." Detective Fyfe looks at me. "It doesn't change a thing, Chris."

"What do you mean?" I blurt out. I feel myself shaking. "Christ, that's only three years older than Devon."

"Chris, look at me." When I finally do, Detective Fyfe says, "It doesn't matter if he was thirteen or thirty. You didn't have a choice. He *did* have a choice. He made a bad one and he paid for it. It's as simple as that."

He takes a deep breath then says in a gentler tone, "This is a tough thing, son, I know. You're not gonna get over it just like that. But you did the best you could. You did the right thing. You keep telling yourself that, because it's true." He takes another breath. "But you need to try to put it behind you. Not only for your sake, but for your family's too. 'Cause you're the man of the house."

He pats me on the shoulder; he might be about to stand up when I suddenly ask, "How well did you know my father? I mean, were you friends?"

Detective Fyfe studies me a moment before he says, "I knew him pretty well. Well enough to be invited to his barbecues. He had a lot of friends on the force. A lot of people liked your dad. He was a good man. As good as they get." He stands up. "Come on. I'll give you a ride home."

"It's not far. I'll walk."

"I said I'm giving you a ride home. Let's go."

We drive the six blocks in silence. In front of my house, as I'm about to get out he says, "Hey." Reaching into his jacket pocket, he pulls out a small card, writes something on the back, then hands it to me. "This has my number at the station on it. I've also written down my cell phone number. If you need something—to talk, anything—you call me, okay? Anytime. Your mother too. Anything she needs. Tell her that for me."

"Okay." I put it into my wallet as he pulls away.

I take a deep breath and wait a minute before going back inside my house. So now I know for sure who the intruder was—and how old he was. Caleb Brannick. Thirteen years old. Dead. If I hadn't gone downstairs, if I had just called the police and waited with Devon until they'd arrived, even if I had just tried to get him out of the house instead of me going into that kitchen, none of this would have happened.

Taking another deep breath, I look up at the window to Devon's room. Maybe I can still go in there and tell him good night.

But I decide it's better just to leave him alone as I go back in through the front door.

9

THEN

The dream came back last night.

"Shoot him! Shoot him!" I'm screaming at Dad. But Dad's moving toward the girl instead, so I lunge for Dad's gun on the floor because if I can get to it before the guy fires, maybe I can save him. The guy's about to shoot, and Dad's almost there, and my fingers are almost touching...

The shooting happened too late to make Friday's edition

of the county rag. But like Detective Fyfe said, there's a story in Saturday's paper. Front page.

LOCAL TEEN SHOOTS INTRUDER

Followed by a basic rundown of what happened. There really isn't much more to it than what Detective Fyfe told me. No mention of any family members other than his mother.

Down the page is a profile of Caleb Brannick, along with a picture of him. He's smiling, and I take a good long look at him. But try as I might, I can't make the picture fit with who I saw bleeding on our kitchen floor.

Mom takes the calls from various news agencies interested in speaking to me. She also drives Devon to his playoff practice. Normally, I take him to all his practices. He's still not talking to me though. Mom says he was fine at practice and so was everyone around him. The collision is forgotten. Devon didn't mean to hurt anyone, everyone says. Not a nice kid like him.

In Sunday's paper, there's an editorial.

The headline reads:

LOCAL TEEN A HERO

I almost don't read it.

By now, just about everyone has heard about what happened in Maple-Braden Township early Friday morning, while most everyone else was sleeping. The kind of life-and-death decision most of us have never faced, and hopefully never will, confronted sixteen-year-old Chris Russo. And the boy faced it head-on. Like a man.

I begin to skim the rest, asking myself why I'm bothering to read it at all, until I come to this:

Chris Russo is the sixteen-year-old son of Michael Thomas Russo, a Maple-Braden police officer who was killed in the line of duty when his oldest son was thirteen, leaving behind his wife, Linda; Chris; and his younger son, Devon. The officer was responding to a domestic dispute. A man with a gun was holding his own daughter hostage. There wasn't time for reinforcements to get there. Perhaps he was tired, since he was several hours into the second of a double shift, and wasn't thinking as clearly as he would have been otherwise. But it is believed that Officer Russo, in hopes of keeping the man from shooting the girl, put his gun down on the ground, breaking one of the cardinal rules of law enforcement—a police officer never relinquishes his weapon. But one thing is known for sure: as more police arrived, the man pulled the trigger and would have killed the girl had Officer Russo not jumped between them and taken the bullet meant for her.

Would it have turned out differently if Russo had held on to his gun?

Perhaps his oldest son was remembering that when he decided to take the gun…

There's more, but I put the paper down midsentence.

Mom, having walked into the room, sighs and says, "He shouldn't have written that about your father."

She fiddles for something in her shirt pocket, makes herself stop. But not before I make out the tip of a cigarette.

"Are you okay?" she asks.

I nod. But I'm not seeing her. Instead, I am seeing the picture of Caleb Brannick in yesterday's paper. Then I see him on the floor, eyes begging me for something, blood pumping.

I still can't make them match.

10

NOW

"That was a good picture of Caleb," Derek says, surprising me. "I didn't know Mom even had any pictures, much less a good one." He looks at me. "That was the first you knew his name? When you saw it in the paper?"

The little finger on my left hand is still cushioned between the blades of the garden shears. But Derek has let up on the pressure. "No, it was when Detective Fyfe told me," I say, hearing the tremble in my voice. "But… seeing it in the paper like that made it more…"

"Real?" he finishes for me after I hesitate.

After a moment, I nod.

He leans back, pulling the garden shears from my finger, which allows me to breathe a little easier. "I read that article," he says. "The writing sucked. He waits till the end to tell everyone that my brother was only thirteen. Like it doesn't matter. What it said about your father... That really happened? Your father died saving that girl?"

"Yes," I say, my voice a hoarse whisper.

"Did he really put his gun down?"

"That's what they say."

"That's rough. You taking over for him like that, that's not easy. Guess you really love your brother to be willing to do that."

"Yes." *Where the hell is he going with this?*

"I loved my brother too, you know," Derek continues. "I wouldn't be doing this if I didn't."

I don't say anything.

"You want some more water?"

"Please."

Derek goes to get it and gives it to me the same as before.

"Better?" he asks.

"Yes," I say. Then I add, "Thank you."

He tosses the empty cup to the side and sits back down. "Sounds like your dad was really into your brother playing baseball. All that attention he gave him… Must've made you jealous."

"No," I say, hesitating. "Not at all."

"Come on. I can hear it in your voice."

"No, really. It just…"

"Just what?" he asks.

"We were different."

"Yeah. He was the favorite son and you weren't. Seems pretty straightforward to me. Happens all the time in families. Not your fault you weren't the athlete your dad wanted."

"I…I tried…"

"To be an athlete? Play baseball?"

I nod.

"But you gave it up."

"Yes."

"How old were you?"

I look at him. "Ten."

"So you were already a disappointment to your dad before your brother started playing baseball."

I open my mouth, then close it.

"Clearly you didn't measure up to the vision Daddy had of the perfect son. Thank God he had Devon, huh?"

"Please stop it."

"Doesn't that piss you off?"

"I told you!" I snap. "We were just different. Had different interests."

Derek stares at me. "Okay, I'll bite. What were you interested in?"

After a moment, I tell him, "School choir."

He almost smiles. "Really? You liked to sing?"

"Yeah."

"Were you any good?"

I don't answer.

"Did your dad like to watch you sing in the choir?"

"Sure."

"I don't know," he says, shaking his head. "You answered that kind of quick. Maybe too quick. You still in choir now?"

I hesitate. "No."

"Why?"

"I stopped."

"You mean you had to stop. To take care of your brother. Did you want to?"

"It was no big deal."

"That's not my question. Did you *want* to stop?" He leans in, waving the garden shears in front of me. "The truth, remember?"

When I don't respond, he lays the flat part of the shears onto my left hand.

"No," I answer finally, my voice a harsh whisper.

"Right," he says, pulling back. "Anything for your brother. Don't talk about what you want, only talk about what little brother wants. Even the last conversation you had with your dad... That's a shame. Really."

I look at him. "What are you talking about?"

Derek looks at me. "It was your last special walk with Daddy before he was killed, and what does he talk about? Your brother. How he's going to get better and better. How great it is he's going to get to play fall ball. What a great kid he is, blah blah blah. I'll bet he did that a lot on your special walks."

"Wait a minute, that's not—"

"And then to make things worse, he got himself killed protecting some kid he doesn't even know, leaving you to hold the bag to do his job. Take care of your brother. Make sure his baseball career's going okay. What a bastard."

"Stop it!" I blurt out. "He's not... You don't have the right—"

"I have *every right*!" Derek suddenly shouts, his spittle dotting my face. "*Your* brother's alive. Mine isn't. Because *you* killed him. That gives me the right to say what the hell I want!" He grabs hold of my little finger again with the blades of the garden shears.

I feel them pressing again. Glancing down, I can see where blood has started to trickle out from under the blades.

"*I'm* in control! We talk about what *I* want to talk about! You were jealous of your brother. Mad at your dad. Mad at him even now, right? Truth, remember? You know the penalty if you lie. The man's using his private time with you, his oldest son, to talk about Devon. Then he dies saving another kid's life. Where did you fit in? When were you going to get your moment? When were you going to become important enough for him to—"

All at once, he starts to cough. It doesn't last as long this time. When he's finished, he leans back, even pulling the garden shears away.

I should keep my mouth shut, but I can't. "What do you care? Why is it so important to you?"

I don't know how he's going to react, and I shut my eyes. When nothing happens, I open them to find him staring at me.

After a long silence, he sighs. "Fathers," he mutters. "They can be a pain sometimes. You should have met my dad; he was a real prick. You're not the only one who had to watch over a younger brother..." He falters.

I wait, expecting him to continue. He says nothing

for a long time. I hate this silence game. Am I supposed to say something now? He's holding the shears in his lap. Maybe he's had a change of heart. Maybe...

And just like that, the blades slide easily back into place.

11

THEN

Monday. My first day back at school since the shooting. I have no idea how my classmates or teachers will act, but I need to be ready. I've thought it through, and if I'm going to get through this, if I'm going to make this work, I have to own it. That means, if people ask, I'm going to talk about it. This is my fault, my responsibility.

It's what Dad would want.

Eating this morning in the dining room instead of the kitchen, Devon is still subdued. He talks to Mom but not to me unless he has to. Something's changed between us, and I'm not sure how to fix it.

"Playoffs start tonight," I try after a bite of Frosted Flakes. Like he doesn't already know that. "Does Coach think you guys are ready for the big game?" I sound inane.

After a moment, he shrugs. "I think so."

"Do *you* think you're ready?"

Silence. Followed by a nod. He continues to stare at his cereal instead of looking at me.

"Did you hit any balls out of the park at Saturday's practice?"

"A couple," he mumbles. He looks at Mom. "May I leave for school a little early? I can play on the playground."

"Sure," she says. "Make sure you brush your teeth first."

"Just give me a minute and I'll be ready to go too," I tell him. I always walk with him in the morning since his school is on the way to the high school; he gets a ride home from Brady's mom in the afternoons.

"I wanna walk by myself," he says at the bottom of the stairs. "I'm big enough."

I stare at him, but he's looking at Mom, not me. "You bet you are," she says after a moment. "That's fine."

He hurries upstairs. I hear the faucet go on in the bathroom.

I say nothing. I'm not sure my voice would work if I tried.

After a moment, Mom says, "I made an appointment

with some professional cleaners. They're coming today to work on the kitchen while I'm at the diner. It'll be done by the time you get home."

The faucet turns off and Devon comes back downstairs. He's got his backpack on, and he goes up to Mom and gives her a hug. "Have a good day," she says, smiling.

He turns and starts out of the room. "Hey, Devon," I call out.

He stops, waits.

"I'll see you after school, okay?"

He nods without looking at me, then leaves the room. I hear the front door open and close a couple seconds later.

I dip my spoon into my cereal and leave it there. Mom says, "Don't take it to heart, Chris. When you were his age, there were times you were so mad at me I was sure you hated me."

I take in a deep, shaky breath. "This is…different."

"No, it's not. I watch him on the baseball field, a head taller than every other kid out there… It's easy to forget he's only ten. But he loves you. More than anybody. More than me, I think."

"That's not true—"

"It is. And that's fine. Did you talk to him like I said?"

"No."

"Then you don't even know what he's mad about."

I look down. "He's mad at me about what happened the other night."

"Why?"

"I think maybe because I didn't stay with him. Because I…"

"Killed somebody?"

I look up at her, surprised.

"If that's the case," she continues, "once he thinks about it, he'll understand."

"Understand what?"

"That sometimes there are things you have to do to protect the ones you love."

I hesitate. Look down again. "He was only thirteen."

"And if you hadn't gone downstairs, and he'd come up and killed you, would it matter then that he was thirteen?" She leans across the table toward me. "Yes, it's a shame he was so young. But you and Devon are alive. That's what matters to me. Devon is ten years old; if he doesn't understand, well, make him understand. Talk to him when he gets home from school today."

"He's got the game—"

"So? Just do it." She takes in another deep breath and stares at me in silence.

"What?" I say finally.

"This is my fault," Mom says. "I should have been here when it happened."

"Mom, it's not—"

She waves me off. "He lost his father way too young, and before I knew it, you had stepped into the role. I haven't told you enough how much it means to me. But I depend on you too much. I forget you're sixteen. You should be out with friends, doing the things teenage boys do. You're too young to be a pseudo-parent. I shouldn't be the one out on dates. You should."

"Mom, stop it. I'm okay. Devon and I will work it out."

Mom reaches across the table to squeeze my hand. "Promise me you'll talk to him when he gets home from school."

"Mom…"

"Promise me."

After a moment, I tell her, "I promise."

"Are you okay?" Terry asks me in the hallway. I'm getting a little tired of him asking me that.

Fifth period. Lunch.

"Everybody's talking about you," Terry says as we walk toward the cafeteria.

"Not to me they aren't," I tell him.

"They probably don't know what to say to you. Doesn't mean they aren't talking."

"Mr. Schubert called me into his office."

"What did Principal Dorko want?"

"I think he just felt he had to 'cause it was his job. He said a lot of kids are probably going to want to talk to me about it, but it was better for me and for everyone if I didn't let it go to my head and stay focused on my schoolwork. If I can't, then maybe I should stay home for a couple days."

"What a dickwad."

"He did say I could talk to the school counselor, if I wanted to."

"Are you going to?"

I shake my head. "I don't see the point."

"I heard Feiler and Baumann talking." Science teacher and English teacher. "Baumann said he totally agrees with what you did."

I get a queasy feeling in my stomach.

"Baumann probably wishes *he* could shoot a few students," Terry continues. "If somebody pointed a gun at him though, I bet he'd piss his pants."

In the cafeteria, we find a table. I pull out my bag lunch.

"Tom Callahan says you should get a medal," Terry offers.

"Really?"

"Bob Reidy says if it had been him in that situation, he wouldn't have waited for the kid to pull a gun."

"Reidy should shut the hell up."

"Chris, you didn't tell me he was only thirteen."

I don't say anything.

"It doesn't matter, you know," he says. "He still tried to...you know."

Is he going to push this?

"How's Devon?" he asks.

The question startles me. "What do you mean?"

"The game. Running into the catcher. It was...I don't know...weird."

"He's fine."

"Like Matt said, he must think you're a hero. The way you stood up for you and him."

Before I can respond, Matt, Eric, and Ben join us. Not just them—they've brought a crowd. Five or six others surround us while Matt sits across from me. Rita Moyer is part of the group. There was a time when seeing her here, showing some interest in what I have to say, would have made me happy. But that was before a month ago, when I finally got up the nerve to ask her out to the spring dance and she said she couldn't go because she had something else that night. Then she ended up going to the dance with Matt. I stayed home with Devon that night so Mom could work a night shift.

"All right, we're here," Matt says.

I look at him. "Here for what?"

"For what?" Matt says, smiling at the rest of the group he's assembled. "Like you don't know you're the big story around here." He leans across the table. "You agreed, remember? To tell us what happened?"

I notice other kids in the cafeteria glancing our way. A few teachers too.

"I didn't know you had it in you," Matt continues. "Like something out of the movies. Bruce Willis kind of shit. You faced the ultimate and you didn't choke. You came through. No one's gonna mess with you now." He grins. "So tell us about it," he says, pulling back and waving his hand to indicate the crowd as if he's a talk show host and I'm the main guest.

"What...do you want to know?" I say finally.

"What was it like? It must have been, I don't know, like being in a video game or something."

I look at him.

"You know. *Call of Duty? Medal of Honor?* Those games are like the real thing."

"I...I don't play those games," I say in a low voice.

"Oh." Matt looks a little annoyed now. He brought these people over to give them a show and I'm not delivering. "Come on, tell us. Was it cool or what?"

I glance up at the group of kids gathered behind him. Most of them would probably pass me by without saying a word to me, but now they're all watching me expectantly, interested in what I have to say. "Yeah," I tell them. "It was cool."

Matt gets a big grin on his face, looking again at the group he's gathered, then back at me. "What was it like to watch him go down?" he asks. "God, it must've felt...I don't know... Did he draw first and you were faster? Was he dead right away? Or did he, you know... take a while?"

The guy is looking at me, shaking, his eyes pleading, like he wants to tell me something but can't.

"I was faster," I say quietly. "And...yes, it took a while."

"Was there a lot of blood?"

The bullet got him in the neck. The blood keeps coming.

"Yeah."

"Jeez. And you...watched him?"

"I called 911."

I notice Terry staring at me. Eyes wide. I haven't even told *him* this much.

"I gotta hand it to you. You've got balls."

"Well, you gotta do what you gotta do."

"That's right," Matt says. "People gotta learn, they mess with you, there are consequences. Listen, I might be having a party this weekend, if I can convince my parents. You wanna come? A lot of other kids wanna hear what really happened. Not the crap they read in the paper or see on the news."

He leans forward again, motioning me to meet him at the middle of the table, his mouth almost to my ear. "I know a couple girls especially would be interested in talking to you." Pulling back once more, he says, "Give me your cell."

"Sure." Feeling as if I'm in a daze, I pull it out and hand it to him.

He pushes buttons on my phone as he talks. "Here's my cell number. In case you wanna do something or just hang out. You know?"

Kids are watching in wonder, and I can tell what they're thinking. Matt Fisher is actually giving Chris Russo his cell phone number. How many of them wish they had the same privilege? I notice Terry staring at us with the same wide-eyed envy.

Matt slides my phone back to me. "Text me so I can have your number." I do, typing "text" on the screen and pressing Send. "Great," he says after hearing the ding from his phone. "Talk to you later." He gets up, nods at the others, and, as if they were waiting for their cue, they move with him.

"Later, Chris," Eric says, patting me on the arm. A few others smile at me as they follow Matt.

"See you guys," Terry says, like he's been friends with them forever. I give them a wave myself, still not sure I believe what just happened.

I notice Rita is one of the last to leave as she stares at me a moment before finally turning away.

"Man, you're in," Terry says after everyone's gone. "You're a celebrity, dude. Inquiring minds wanna know. You'll be able to milk this for a *long* time."

I just shrug.

"You're going."

He means to the party. "I'll have to check with Mom, make sure she doesn't need me to stay with Devon."

"You're kidding, right? Let *her* stay with Devon."

When I don't respond, he asks, "You okay?"

I look at him. "I'm fine," I tell him, putting a little edge to my voice. "Why do you keep asking me that?"

"Sorry. I've just never seen you act like... Sorry." Terry stands up, his lunch tray in hand, and says, "I'm gonna see if they've got any of those brownies left. I'll get you one. My treat."

He walks away, and for the moment, I'm alone. And it feels...I don't know...better than it felt a few minutes ago with everybody standing around expecting something from me, even if part of me enjoyed getting all that attention. It's hard to explain, even to myself. I consider getting up and leaving before Terry gets back, but when I turn, I see Rita standing there staring at me, looking great as always, I have to admit, with her light-brown hair pulled back and her face always looking like she just scrubbed it. Looking great, except for the angry expression on her face.

"I...I think..." she says, fidgeting. "I think what you just did was awful."

Her comment catches me off guard.

"How can you sit there telling people about it, all the gory details, like it's some great story? Like it was just an adventure you had, like what happened was nothing?"

I can't think of anything to say, so I just sit here, waiting for her to continue.

"Do you think you're special now? A star? Why don't you get Mr. Schubert to give you the auditorium for a period. You can tell the whole school how exciting it was, sign autographs afterward."

"I—"

"You know, I'm glad I didn't go to the dance with you last month."

Why the hell would she bring that up?

"I wouldn't say yes to you if you were the only guy on earth—"

"So why didn't you just leave?" I hear myself saying, cutting her off.

She looks at me, surprised. "What?"

"You stayed like everybody else. If what I had to say bothered you so much, why didn't you leave?"

I'm not sure where my words are coming from, but they seem to have shut her up. She keeps opening her mouth, then closing it.

A part of me is saying I should shut up now. But my words keep coming. "In fact, why'd you come over with everybody in the first place? Must have been a little curious about the gory details, I guess."

Abruptly, she turns and walks away quickly, almost knocking into Terry, who's coming back eating a brownie, another one in his hand.

Terry reaches the table. "What'd she want?" he asks with a glint in his eye.

"I gotta get to my locker," I say, standing up.

"You're not gonna tell me? Your best friend?"

The look I give him makes him back up.

"Hey, I didn't mean… You want this brownie?"

I know I shouldn't be snapping at him like this; he's

my best friend. Maybe my only friend. But I'm too irritated by my conversation with Rita to do any more than turn and head for the exit. I sense him hesitating behind me a moment before following me like a hurt puppy.

12

THEN

Terry has band practice after school on Mondays, so I walk home alone. Not that he would want to walk with me, the way I've been treating him lately. I should say something to him. Tomorrow.

I've gone two blocks when I hear, "You're right. I was curious."

Turning, I see Rita stepping out from behind a mailbox, as if she's been waiting for me. "I let Matt and them talk me into going over to you, and by the time you were finished, I was mad at myself for agreeing to go and for listening, so I took it out on you. I'm sorry for snapping at you the way I did."

I stare at her a moment, not sure how to respond.

I guess I take a little too long because she nods and says, "Okay, well, I just wanted to tell you that," and starts to turn away.

"I never said it was *nothing*," I hear myself say.

She turns back. "What?"

"You said I was talking like what happened was nothing. But I never said it was nothing."

"I said I'm sorry."

"And I didn't ask for it. I wish it hadn't happened at all."

"But you said it was cool."

"What am I supposed to say?" I ask. "Do you think Matt and them want to hear that I was scared? And wishing I hadn't gone downstairs in the first place?"

"If that's the truth."

"They don't want to hear the truth." Suddenly, I don't like the direction this is going.

"But you liked it, right? All the attention?"

"I'm sorry for what I said to you before," I tell her. "It was uncalled for. I've gotta go."

"You can tell *me* the truth," Rita says, surprising me.

I stare at her.

"If you want to...I mean."

I look down. Part of me is telling myself to walk away.

Truth, she says? Like telling me she couldn't go to the dance when really she just didn't want to go with *me*? Why should I tell her the truth? Why should I care what she thinks?

But this whole conversation is freaking weird. Like an alien or something has taken over my body, making me stay here and talk to her.

"What happened to you," Rita says, "having to shoot someone, I don't know what I'd do if—"

I cut her off. "I really...don't want to talk about it anymore. Is that okay?"

"Sure," she says. Then she hesitates before asking, "Are you heading home? Can I walk with you?"

I shrug. "If you want to."

She comes forward until she's next to me, and we begin walking. "What would you...*like* to talk about?"

"Just not..." I respond.

She nods.

For the next three blocks, we walk in silence. Maybe it's going to be like this the whole way. Maybe nobody's going to be able to talk to me about anything else ever again.

"How do you think you did on Gallagher's test?" Rita asks.

"All right, I guess. There was a lot more from the textbook than I thought there'd be."

"Did you read the chapters?"

"A couple times."

"I crammed it all in last night. Had all weekend but I waited until the last minute."

"Do you think you passed?"

"Passed, yes. Did well?" She shrugged. "Now I'm really going to have to ace the final if I'm going to keep my A."

"I'm happy if I get a B in that class."

"My parents would flip out if I only got a B."

We walk on for another block or so.

Suddenly, Rita surprises me with, "I'm sorry I didn't say yes when you asked me to the dance."

Her abrupt apology makes me stop. She turns around to face me. "I've felt bad about it ever since," she says.

"Not bad enough to keep yourself from going out with Matt a couple more times after the dance," I snap back.

From the look she gives me, I'm not sure if she's going to slap me or just walk away in a huff. Instead, she surprises me again by taking a breath and saying, "I probably deserved that. I don't know what you heard about me and Matt, but I only went out with him two more times after the dance. I'm not sure what he's said about us—what I've heard is just his BS—but there was nothing between us. A couple dates. That's it."

In the awkward silence that follows, we both look away. I'm not sure how I'm supposed to respond.

"Well," she says, glancing in the direction of her house, "I've been wanting to tell you that. I guess I better—"

"Why did you lie to me?" I hear myself ask. Now I'm the one with surprises. "You told me you couldn't go. If Matt had already asked you, you could've just told me that." Like I said, this conversation is freaking weird.

"He didn't," she says after a moment, head down. "I mean he hadn't yet."

"So it wasn't that you couldn't go," I say. "You didn't want to go. With me."

"But I thought there was a chance he might..." She sighs. "Oh, hell. Truth, right? I just didn't want to go with you. So shoot me. It's nothing personal. You seem like a nice guy and I knew you had a crush on me."

I look at her. "You did? I mean, you thought I had a crush on you?"

"Come on, you did. I knew you did. It was obvious. Look, I'm sorry. You weren't on my radar, okay? Matt Fisher seemed to be interested in me. *The* Matt Fisher. There were a couple of other boys I thought might ask me out too if he didn't. You weren't one of them. When you asked, I...I panicked. Made up something to say I couldn't go. And then Matt did ask me..."

"So you got what you wanted," I say softly.

"I thought so," she says, grimacing. "Mr. Popular, Mr. Handsome. Yeah, I went out with him a couple more times. I thought that was what you did with someone like him. Big mistake. As far as he's concerned, everything's about him. It's not fun, believe me."

Another awkward silence. Then she looks at me again and says, "You want to say good-bye now and never talk to me again, I'd understand. But it's true what I said. I've always felt bad about what I said to you. So we could try again."

I look back at her. "What do you mean?"

"There's Matt's party this Saturday," she says.

"Won't Matt have a problem with me bringing you?"

"He's moved on, believe me."

"He may not even have the party."

"He will. His parents never refuse him anything."

I shrug. "Okay."

"Okay...?"

"Okay, if you say he's having the party, I guess he is."

"Hey, if you don't want to take me—"

"No, I...I do."

"You do?"

I look at her.

She steps toward me. "But...you're mad at me?"

"No. Well, maybe a little. You did say you wouldn't go out with me if I was the only—"

"Shut up," she says, but she's smiling. I smile back.

"They're gonna want to talk to me about...you know," I add. "Is that okay with you?"

"Maybe we can just make an appearance then go somewhere else."

"Okay. But I...I have to check... My mother might have to work and then I'd have to watch Devon."

"Your brother, right?"

I nod. "He's ten."

"She can't get a sitter?"

"We really can't afford... I'm usually the one to..."

"I get it," she says quietly. "It's nice, you taking care of your little brother like that. I guess we don't have to go to the party if your mom needs you. If you don't mind me helping you watch your brother."

I look at her. "No. I...I wouldn't."

"Good. So, are you asking me to the party?"

My heart does little flutters. "Sure. I mean, yes."

Rita smiles. "I accept." She turns. "This is my street."

"Right. I'll see you later. Tomorrow."

"Yes, you will." Rita puts her hand on mine. "You're kind of funny, you know?"

"Funny?" I say.

"In a good way. Really." She lets her hand linger for a moment. Then, as if suddenly aware of what she's doing, Rita pulls away and moves off down her street. After a few steps though, she looks back over her shoulder to wave at me. She's smiling.

I wave back.

Like I said, a weird conversation. But a good one.

My heart is still fluttering as I keep walking.

13

NOW

"So killing my brother got you a girlfriend," Derek growls. "And some new friends." He sounds like he might start coughing again any minute.

"It wasn't like that." The garden shears are still in place, but at least he hasn't increased the pressure.

"It wasn't? Suddenly you're Mr. Popular after showing everybody what a badass you are. And all it took was my brother's *life!*"

I don't know what to say. I expect the blades to start shredding my flesh any minute now.

He leans in. "You told them killing my brother was

cool," he hisses, his voice a thin rasp.

"I said it because I knew it was what Matt and the others wanted to hear."

"You sure about that?"

"Yes." My gaze is still on the shears.

"Look at me!"

My eyes dart up.

"Tell me the truth," he says. "You liked Matt talking to you in front of everybody like that, treating you like you're one of the *cool* kids."

"I…"

"What?"

My mouth is dry again, and I swallow. "You're right," I say. "I did like it."

"And you liked Rita talking to you, right? Showing interest? Even if she did treat you like crap before."

I feel the pressure from the blades where the blood from before has dried. "She explained that," I whisper against the pain.

"Do you think she would've given you the time of day if you didn't have such a tough-guy story to tell?"

My eyes are still on the garden shears. "Maybe not. I…I don't know." I look at him. "Did you hurt her?"

"What do you mean?" He stares back at me.

"Before you grabbed me at her house… Rita was

opening the door. Did she see you? Did you hurt her?"

"Why? It's not like you can do anything about it."

Bastard! Suddenly, I want to grab him, make him tell me what he did to her. See how he likes knowing he could lose a finger any minute. But he's right. There's nothing I can do. Not right now. He's still staring at me as he slowly tightens his grip on the shears.

"Keep going," he says.

14

THEN

I get home thinking about my promise to Mom this morning.

Promise me you'll talk to him.

Less than five minutes later, the phone rings.

"I just called to see how you're doing," I hear Detective Fyfe say.

"I'm okay," I tell him, surprised by his call.

"I guess you read the articles in the paper over the weekend."

"Yeah."

"What he said about your father... It was unnecessary."

"Nothing I haven't heard already, Detective Fyfe."

"I guess that's true. Hey, call me Bob."

I hesitate. "All right."

"Are reporters still trying to talk to you?"

"They've backed off."

"Good."

The silence on the other end grows heavy. I glance at the clock. Devon will be home in less than twenty minutes.

"Well, as long you're okay," Detective—I mean Bob—finally says.

"Did my dad...?"

Silence on the other end. He's waiting for me to continue. But what am I trying to say?

"What about him, Chris?" he says finally.

It feels, again, as if some other voice has taken me over, trying to keep this man on the phone. This man who knew my father in ways I never did.

The question is out of my mouth before I know I'm going to ask it. "Did my dad ever shoot anyone? On the job?"

After a moment, Detective Fyfe says, "No."

"Did you?"

"No. Most cops don't ever pull their guns. All that crap on TV is just that."

"What it said in the article—do you think if my dad hadn't given up his gun...?"

I don't let myself finish the question. But in my head I have another one.

When Dad took the bullet for that girl, was he thinking of me and Devon and what it would mean to the two of us to lose our father?

Several long seconds go by before Detective Fyfe—I can't get myself to call him Bob—responds. "He died doing his job," he says. "Protecting people. That's what we do. He saved that little girl's life. That means something. Something you'll always know about him. Something you can tell your own kids when you tell them about their grandfather. Whenever you *honor* him. You'll know that your father was a hero."

"The man who killed him," I say in a quiet voice, "died in prison, didn't he?"

"Yes," Detective Fyfe says. "That was justice, son."

Don't worry, Chris. The punk who did this is gonna pay.

"I'd better go," I say. "Devon's gonna be home soon."

"Is Devon doing okay?"

I hesitate. "Yes."

"He's very lucky to have you for an older brother."

I feel my stomach twisting into another knot.

"Tell him I said hi. Your mom too."

"Sure." I watch my hand return the phone to the cradle. Devon comes home ten minutes later. He usually has a hug for me but not this time. I'm going to talk to him, I tell myself. But I forgot about the social studies project he's been working on that is due tomorrow, and it turns out he's got math, spelling, and reading, all of which he needs to work on right away, with his game in a couple of hours.

"Okay," I tell him. "I don't have a lot of homework, so when you're ready, I'll help you warm up."

"I might just throw against the wall," he says in a low voice, looking down.

I always help him warm up. My heart thumps so hard it hurts. "Need any help with your homework?"

"No, I'm okay." He takes his snack and backpack upstairs to his room.

It seems to take longer for him to finish his homework than it should. When he comes downstairs, we have half an hour until we need to leave for the game. I insist on throwing to him in the backyard as we usually do before a game, but within a few minutes, it's clear he's not into it. He lets easy ground balls get by him and doesn't go after lazy fly balls. Is it because he's still pissed at me? Or is it more than that? I don't want to distract him from his game. We can talk tonight.

I lie and tell Devon there's something inside I forgot to do, go ahead and throw against the wall if he wants.

Mom arrives home a little later than usual, five minutes before we have to leave. On game nights, I often grab dinner from the snack bar at the field; Devon, having eaten a snack, eats after the game. Devon gets in the backseat first. Normally before a game like this, he's all excited and chirping away, but not now. He just sits in the backseat, saying nothing.

Mom asks in a low voice, "Did you talk to him?"

"Not yet," I tell her.

She frowns and gets in behind the wheel. He'll be better once he gets there.

He jumps out of the car at the ball field before we've even come to a complete stop. "Have a good game, sweetheart," Mom calls to him. He waves back. Coach Neville greets him with his usual enthusiasm. I watch Devon carefully. He's smiling. *A good sign*, I tell myself.

On the bleachers, Terry comes over and sits next to me. "Big game tonight," he says, stating the obvious. "Devon up for it?"

"Why wouldn't he be?" I growl.

Terry frowns, says nothing.

We sit in silence for a moment. Then Terry leans in and says in a low voice, "Glad you're going to the party. I am too."

"Party? What party?" Mom asks.

I frown at Terry before turning to her. "A kid at school invited me."

"Do I know him?" Mom asks.

"His name's Matt. It's this Saturday. But I don't know…"

"Are his parents gonna be there?"

"I think so."

"You should go. I'll watch Devon."

"You don't have a date?"

"I'm not seeing that guy anymore."

"Why not?"

"Doesn't matter. I'll watch Devon. You go to the party."

"I don't know if I will go."

"Go. I trust you."

"I'll think about it," I tell her after a moment.

Mom looks at me, frowning, then turns toward the field. "Whatever. But I'm taking Devon to a movie that night. And you're not invited."

Turning, I give Terry an irritated look. Then I stand, announcing, "I'm getting a hot dog. You want something, Mom?"

"Maybe later."

Terry and I climb down off the bleachers. As soon as we're clear, Terry says, "Great. You can go."

"I haven't decided yet."

"But your mom said—"

"I know."

"But you're taking Rita."

I look at him. "Where'd you hear that?"

"Come on, news like that isn't gonna stay secret for long. She's hot."

We walk in silence for a few seconds.

"Hey, she isn't the only girl who would go out with you now if you asked."

I don't say anything.

"Hey, are…are you okay?"

"When are you gonna stop asking me that?"

Terry just gives me a wounded look and says nothing.

At the snack bar, we each get a hot dog and a bottle of water. Like last time, Mrs. Wheat doesn't charge me.

"Jeez," Terry says, "if I'd known all I had to do was shoot someone to get free food…"

I decide to ignore his lame joke.

We stop at the fence, watch the boys warm up. Brady fields a grounder, throws it to Devon at first. It ticks off Devon's glove. Devon didn't try very hard. Or am I just imagining it?

"Brady's so excited about this game, he couldn't eat," Terry says. "They lose this, it's over."

"They'll still be playing baseball. They'll both be on the tournament team," I say.

"Still..." A few minutes of silence pass before Terry blurts out, "Are you mad at me? Is that why you didn't tell me about Rita?"

"Mad about what?"

"For, I don't know, always asking, 'Are you all right?' For telling Matt and them it was okay to talk to you about it. For making that lame joke at the snack bar just now. For everything. Like a jerk, I've been saying the wrong thing all the time—I can tell from the way you look at me—when I should be, I don't know, a better friend. Doing something to help you. I'm sorry, Chris. I can't imagine what it's like, what happened to you. But you know, really...if you need to talk about it...about anything..."

I feel like a schmuck as I turn to him. "It's okay," I tell him. What have I been doing, treating him like this? Sure, he acts like a big puppy dog sometimes, but he really is my best friend. We were eight years old when I helped Terry rebuild his fort after some bullies tore it down because he was the new kid in the neighborhood, and we officially declared ourselves best friends forever. He was with me when I was nine and fell off my bike, scraping my knee, and didn't say a word about me crying like a baby. He was with me when I broke my ankle four years ago just stepping off a curb and he half carried me all the way home to my mom and dad. "I've been the jerk," I say. "All you've been doing since this happened is trying to help me, and I've been treating you like shit. I'm sorry, Terry. I really am. It's just... I've never dealt with something like this. A lot of times I don't know what to do or say when people ask about it. And I worry a lot about Devon. About whether I'm there for him enough...ever since Dad died..." I stop, surprised to hear myself choking up.

"Hey, no problem. Best friends forever," Terry says, quoting the words our eight-year-old selves chanted right after we had finished rebuilding the fort. "And, as for Devon, are you kidding? He couldn't ask for a better brother. He loves you more than anything."

"Do you really think that's true?" I want to ask. But then I hear, "Hey, Chris," and as I turn, Matt slaps me on the back, grinning. Eric and Ben are with him. "We thought we'd come and watch your brother play."

I hesitate. "Sure," I say with a shrug.

"You doing anything after the game?"

"I'm going to have to get him home."

"Your mom can't do that? Come on, Chris, let loose a little."

"It's a school night..."

"Right, right. A school night." He rolls his eyes. "At least tell us how you bagged Rita for my party."

When I look at him, he says, "Hey, she and I had our fling; I've moved on. She's all yours." He leans in again. "Of course, if you want any tips on what she likes, talk to me before Saturday." He motions to the others. "Come on, let's do this right. Let's get a dog. Go White Sox!"

They walk away, toward the snack bar.

We hear Coach Neville call the White Sox in. The game is going to start in a few minutes.

I turn back to Terry, feeling like I should say more. "You sitting with them?" he asks before I can.

"No. With my mom, as usual."

"See you around the third inning."

As he begins to turn, I say, "Hey, Terry, I think I'm doing okay...well, the best I can. But if you're worried about me, you can ask me how I'm doing anytime you want. Okay?"

"Sure, Chris," he says, offering me a lame thumbs-up that makes me smile and his goofy puppy-dog grin. "See you in the third." He turns and heads toward the bleachers. Watching the team head into the dugout, I notice Devon moving slowly, his head down, while most of his teammates run in, passing him by. I consider saying something to him, but I let it go.

As I turn toward the bleachers, I hear a voice behind me. "Chris? Chris Russo?"

15

NOW

"Why'd you stop?" Derek asks.

"Well, I...I figured you know this part. It was you behind me. It was when I met you."

He stares at me, and for the first time, he actually smiles. "I'd be interested in hearing your impression of me. Don't worry. You're not going to hurt my feelings. Just don't lie," he adds, his smile dropping only a little.

16

THEN

"Chris? Chris Russo?"

Who is it this time? I turn back, irritated.

I don't recognize the guy facing me. About my age, I guess, maybe a year older. He definitely doesn't go to Maple-Braden High. Maybe the Catholic school; otherwise, why would he be here at one of our Little League games if he lives in another township? I notice he has two broken teeth in front, one each on top and bottom.

"May I talk to you a minute?" he asks. His voice is rough, raspy, like he needs to clear it. There's a noticeable scar on his neck, near his Adam's apple, so maybe there's actually something wrong with his voice. Besides his broken teeth, I notice his nose looks crooked, like he broke it and it didn't heal straight. Looking more closely, maybe he's older than I first thought.

"This will only take a minute." He doesn't even try to clear his throat, though he does take a second to swallow, which seems difficult.

The White Sox take the field, Devon trotting out to his position at first base. "Look," I say, "I really have to—"

"My name is Derek Brannick."

Hearing that last name makes me stop. I stare at him, my mouth still open.

"Caleb is—was—my brother."

Everything else seems to disappear for a moment. Again, I can see his name and face in the paper. Caleb *Brannick*. The article had only mentioned his mother. No mention at all of a brother.

Christ, what do I say? "I…I'm sorry…"

He puts his hand up. "I'm not here for that," he says. "Actually, I'm not sure why I'm here. I just…" Another swallow. "I know this seems weird. But…can you and I talk? Please? I know you can't now. Not here. Another time. I hadn't seen my brother in a long time. You were literally the last person to see him…"

I glance around the field and bleachers. Nobody seems to be looking in our direction.

"I have questions," he says. "That's all. You see, I'm trying to figure out why he...why Caleb would..."

Behind me, I hear the umpire shout, "Play ball!" The game's starting, but I remain riveted to this spot. I can't move; I'm *afraid* to move.

"I'm sorry," he says. "I shouldn't be... You want to watch your brother play." He gives me a hesitant smile, accenting his broken teeth, before looking out at the field. "Your brother's the big kid out there, right? Bigger than all of them? Strong? Hits all those home runs? Devon, right?"

When I don't respond, he says, "I don't mean to freak you out. I heard people in the stands talking. Some of them were saying they hoped he hits a couple today. This is a big game, right? First round of the playoffs?" Again he swallows. "Caleb never played baseball. Soccer was his game. Well, not *his* game; he played it a little bit when he was younger. Not as talented an athlete as I'm hearing your brother is, but I still liked watching him play back then."

This whole thing feels surreal. He doesn't want an apology; he wants to talk. What does that mean? At least there are a lot of people around. If he was thinking of trying something...

"Look, I'm really sorry about what happened," I tell him. "I wish I could—"

"I told you," he says sharply, his voice sounding like the inside of his throat had been rubbed with sandpaper, "I'm not here for that!" He starts to cough but manages to cut it off. Then he notices my reaction and says, "I didn't mean to raise my voice. Look, I shouldn't have come here. This isn't the right place. You shouldn't have to... Here." He pulls from a pocket what looks like a business card. "This is just something I picked up in a grocery store. But I put my name and cell phone number on the back. Here, take it."

I pull it from his outstretched hand reluctantly. On the front is an advertisement for Clip Clop the Clown, available for parties, with a phone number and email address. But on the other side is another phone number, handwritten in pen.

"It's up to you, okay?" he says reluctantly. "If we can just talk some time. Please. Call me. If you don't want to...then don't. I'll understand. I will. At least I can say I tried." As he turns, he looks back and motions at the field. "I hope Devon has a good game. Hope they win."

Before he gets too far, I call out, "Hey!" He stops, looks at me. "Do you go to one of the other schools around here?"

17

NOW

Derek seems about to say something, but his voice catches, followed by that awful coughing. When he's finished, he leans back and sighs. Shakes his head in frustration. "Damn it," he says, "this voice of mine." He fingers the scar on his throat. "You noticed this right away, huh? It happened in prison. Excuse me, 'juvenile detention.'"

Did he just say prison? I didn't think I could feel any more scared, but hearing him say that sends fresh chills through me.

"A couple of kids decided they didn't like me," Derek

"I dropped out a while back." He gives me a crook
smile. "You're wondering how old I am, aren't you? I
seventeen." He shrugs. "I look beat up, I know."

"I didn't mean…" But actually, he's right. I was wo
dering. I hold up the card. "Maybe I will call."

"I'd appreciate it." He turns and walks toward on
the field complex exits, shoulders slumped, head do

I look again at the card with his cell phone nun
on it. I can hear Detective Fyfe's voice in my head te
me, *What are you doing? Throw it away!* Instead, I
it in my jeans pocket.

continues. "Beat me up. Doctor did his best with the surgery, but I still ended up with permanent damage to my vocal chords. Still haven't been able to get used to talking like this. I'm seventeen and I sound like an old man." He coughs again. Lets out a breath. "Focus," he tells himself. The garden shears pull away, and I try not to breathe too obvious a sigh of relief.

"I guess you have a right to know," he says. "It's been a couple months since I got out. While I was in there, this counselor took interest in me. Still don't know why. He talked to me a lot about the importance of forgiveness. Not about people forgiving *me* for what *I* did. And, believe me, I've done stuff. He talked about forgiving those who hurt *me*. My father and mother mostly. He said that's why I was so angry all the time. He said if I was going to move forward, I had to forgive them.

"It didn't make a lot of sense to me. I'm not sure I get it now. But he would tell me I needed to forgive for *my* sake, not my parents. My anger controlled me. Made me...do things. He said if I could stop blaming them, then I could start taking responsibility for my own actions and start forgiving *myself*. That's what he told me. Sounds stupid, doesn't it?"

He looks at me. "I know I look like crap. Drugs and alcohol and prison'll do that to you. Those things adults tell us we shouldn't do—they're right. I look at you, a year younger than me, and I think, *Did I ever look like that?* People look at you and they see someone with a whole life ahead of them. They look at me, they see someone who screwed up big time, and if I died tomorrow, nobody would care."

Why is he telling me this? I keep quiet.

After a moment, he says, "When I finally got out, I wanted to make up for the mistakes I'd made. Well, one very bad mistake. I had to fix what I did to my little brother. I'm not sure I care about the rest. I had to get him out of our parents' house.

"It's clear you care about your brother. Your father died, and you stepped up. Well, I used to watch out for my brother. Our parents sure didn't. But when I reached fifteen, I couldn't take living there anymore, and I… left. Left him there with *them*. Our parents. He was only eleven years old. Defenseless. I was always better at dealing with them than he was. It must have been awful for him. And I knew what they were doing to him with me no longer home. But I still stayed away. Thought only of myself. Ended up in juvenile detention right after I turned sixteen. Did over a year."

He stops, takes a breath. "A few months before my prison term was scheduled to end, Caleb came to see me. By himself. It's the only time anyone from my family visited me while I was in there. He told me how bad it was. The worst it had ever been. Said he was thinking of running away. I told him if he could just stick it out four more months, I'd come get him and we'd go somewhere together, away from them. I told him to hang in there, that it was going to be all right. I actually said that. *It's going to be all right.*

"When I got out, they actually released me to my mother. Turns out Dad had left, said he didn't want to be living with an ex-con. I figured that was a good thing. But *Caleb* was gone too. Paper said he'd run away, but she'd kicked him out. Figured good riddance. And good riddance to me too. She wanted me out ASAP. She needed a 'fresh start.' Can you believe that? *A fresh start.* I can understand her not wanting anything to do with *me*. But Caleb, he didn't do anything wrong. I'm sure of it. That day he came to see me, he was still the same sweet kid he always was, despite everything. Not like me at all.

"I looked for him. But I had no idea where he was. There was no one to take him, no real friends. All we'd had was…each other. He had to be living on the street, and I tried to find him, I did. But it was hard, and I told myself I had to get…situated somewhere first, make sure

I had a place to bring him to. It took some time, finding someplace that would work for both of us. But I did it. I even got a decent job. But I still couldn't find him.

"And then I read in the paper…in the *paper*…that he's been killed…" Derek stops again, his voice faltering.

I wait, but he says nothing. He stares but not at me.

Finally, he sighs, and his gaze shifts to me. "I didn't want to do this to you. But put yourself in my shoes. How would you feel if your brother was suddenly dead? You'd want to know why. You'd want to know everything. I've listened to you so far, and I think…there's something I'm missing. Or something you're not telling me. If that's true, if you're leaving something out…"

I hold my breath. Waiting. Preparing myself. Imagining how it would affect my life to live without a finger or two. Because no way am I going to tell him…

"Go on," he says abruptly.

18

THEN

A crack of the bat makes me turn and hurry back to my seat. The opposing team, the Blue Jays, have already made a couple of outs by the time I sit down next to Mom.

"Where've you been?" she asks.

"Talking to Terry."

"I saw him with his parents five minutes ago."

"I was talking to other people too." I'm definitely not going to tell her about my conversation with Derek Brannick.

"He look all right to you?" Mom asks, talking about Devon.

He's in position at first base, bent at the knees, glove extended, the way coaches over the years have taught him. I look for that familiar intensity he gets in his eyes when he's playing.

"He's fine," I tell her. I glance back over my shoulder. I see Matt and the others leaving the complex. So much for staying to watch Devon play. I see no sign of Derek Brannick. I feel better that he left, but my heart is still pounding. I turn back and find Mom staring at me.

"You all right?" she asks.

"Yeah." I lean forward to focus on the game.

The Blue Jays make their last out. Bottom of the first, Devon comes up, batting in his usual cleanup spot, with two outs and Brady on first base. First pitch looks like it might have been a little outside, but the umpire calls it a strike. Devon lets the next two pitches go by as well. A ball, then another strike. Finally, he takes a swing at a ball above his head and misses. Strike three.

"It's okay, buddy," I call out to him. "You'll get it next time."

He takes his glove out to first base, throws grounders to the other fielders while the pitcher warms up. I watch him carefully. He seems okay now.

Top of the fourth, it's still scoreless. The Blue Jays

have two outs with a runner on third, but all the White Sox have to do is get the out at first to end the inning.

Which is what it looks like they're going to do. The second baseman grabs the ball grounded to him. Throws it to Devon at first.

It's an easy toss. Right there. And Devon drops it. Clinking off his glove, it lands at his feet. Runner safe. Devon scoops the ball into his glove, head down, while the other team in their dugout and Blue Jays fans in the stands cheer.

The inning ends with the score 1–0.

By the end of the fourth inning, I'm convinced something's wrong. This isn't just Devon having a bad game. He's up third in the inning, and after Brady and the batter following him get on, Devon walks to the plate with runners on first and second and nobody out.

He swings and misses at the first two pitches. Halfhearted swings. Neither pitch was over the plate.

On the next pitch, he hits a weak grounder to the pitcher, and the Blue Jays get a double play at second and first.

Mom stirs next to me. "Just not his game so far, is it?" I watch Coach Neville talk to Devon in the dugout.

By the time we get to the bottom of the sixth inning, we're behind 5–0. Our last chance. We're near the bottom of our order; two batters, then the top of the order will come up. Terry, as usual, is sitting next to me at this point, muttering under his breath.

The Blue Jays bring in a new pitcher. I recognize him. He's good, throws hard.

This kid usually throws strikes, so it's obvious he doesn't have his best stuff when he walks our first two batters. Soon the White Sox have done it again, kept the inning going so that Devon comes to the plate representing the winning run. The score is 5–3 with runners at second and third. One out.

Devon lives for these moments. He loves the challenge.

I watch him carefully, study his body language. He seems okay. Focused. Maybe talking to the coach helped.

I can feel the White Sox fans in the bleachers stirring. Excited. Some people shout encouragement to Devon. Kids have gathered on the other side of the outfield wall, as usual, anticipating a home run.

Take a deep breath, I try to tell him mentally. *You don't have to hit a home run. Just keep the rally going. Even a ground out would bring in a run.*

As Devon sets himself, I see the catcher move his glove outside. *Way* outside. The first pitch hits the glove. Ball one. The catcher might as well stand up as they do in Major League Baseball. The second pitch is just as far outside. They're intentionally walking him. The other team's coach would rather put the winning run on base than face Devon in this situation.

The third ball goes by. Three balls, no strikes. I lean back, frustrated. Mom looks at me. "They're doing that on purpose," she says. "Can they do that?"

"Sure they can," I mutter angrily. At least the White Sox will have the bases loaded with only one out.

The pitcher looks at the runners. The catcher extends his glove again. Devon waits to take his walk.

The ball comes down a foot wide of the plate.

And Devon swings. Misses.

I can't believe it. What was he thinking? Maybe he's frustrated too. Wants to get the big hit. Figured he'd try one swing. Now he'll let the next wide one go by.

But he doesn't. Even though the ball is even more outside. He swings. Misses by a lot.

Full count. What's going on?

Devon. Take the walk. Except maybe they're not going to walk him now, not with two strikes on him. Maybe they'll give him a pitch to hit. Is that why he did it? Force them now to try and get him out? Give him one pitch he can drive?

I try to see Devon's face, get an idea what he's thinking.

His face has no expression. Blank.

Devon waits, bat ready. The pitcher takes in a deep breath, exhales, brings his glove to his chest, checks the runners. This time the catcher's glove does not move outside.

The sound in the stands has grown muted. Everyone knows what Devon is capable of.

The pitcher winds up. Releases the ball.

It comes straight down the middle of the plate. A perfect pitch to drive. I can see the catcher doing everything he can short of jumping across the plate to grab it before Devon swings.

But my brother lets it go by. The sound of the ball slapping the catcher's glove fills the air.

"Strike three!" the umpire calls.

White Sox fans groan while Blue Jays fans cheer. I hear Terry whisper in an unbelieving voice, "How could he let that go by?"

Devon turns away from the plate. His body language reveals nothing.

But for just a brief moment, he looks up into the stands. At me.

His eyes are narrow. Gray slate. His brow is furrowed. I've seen that look on his face two other times in his life.

The last time was during the previous game, as he

went barreling home from third, against his coach's orders, and slammed into the catcher.

Only now the expression is directed right at me.

I hear Mom let out a deep sigh and say, in a low voice, "He just doesn't have it today."

I don't respond. I'm still watching Devon, now sitting at one end of the dugout, away from his teammates.

The rest of the game ends quickly.

But not in the way I expect.

Maybe the pitcher is so ecstatic over striking out our best hitter in that situation—especially when he was trying to walk him—that he let his guard down. Our next batter, on the very next pitch, a kid named Jake Holohan, makes the first home run he's hit this year count big time, sending it sailing over the right field wall. And just like that, the game is over. Final score: White Sox 6, Blue Jays 5. The White Sox will be moving on to the next round of the playoffs.

The Blue Jays walk off the field, dejected. Jake's teammates mob him when he reaches home plate. The last one to join them is Devon.

19

THEN

Normally, we'd stop at Dairy Queen after a victory like this, but Devon says he's not hungry. Mom tries to talk him into it but only gets one-syllable responses, and eventually, she gives up. I sit in the front seat, fuming.

Devon goes right upstairs as soon as we enter the house. We hear his door close.

"Christ, you'd think they lost," Mom says.

I march toward the stairs.

"Where are you going?" Mom asks.

"To talk to him."

"Do you think that's a good idea?"

"I thought you *wanted* me to talk to him."

"Maybe not now. He's obviously upset."

I start up.

"Chris, it's just a game."

"It's not just the game."

"Chris—"

"Mom, I'm doing this!" I continue up the stairs without looking back. She gives up trying to stop me.

I find Devon on his bed, still in uniform, with his Nintendo DS in his hand, the familiar sounds of the Mario brothers coming from it.

"I want to talk to you," I say.

His fingers keep working the buttons.

"Turn that off!"

"I'm in the middle of a game."

"*Now*, Devon!"

Sighing, he closes the DS and tosses it on the bed. He waits, not looking at me.

"What's going on with you?"

He shrugs. "Nothing."

"What were you doing in that game?"

He shrugs again.

"You weren't even trying."

"I had a bad game."

"*Bullshit!*" I rarely curse in front of my brother,

and it makes him look at me. "That last at bat, what were you doing?" I continue, growing angrier. "They were *trying* to walk you. I saw the way you looked at me. You weren't just having a bad game. You did it on purpose! Why? If you're mad at me, then have the guts to tell me to my face so we can talk about it. Don't take it out on your teammates when they're counting on you."

He looks away. Says nothing. I can see he's fighting tears. "Maybe I don't want to play baseball anymore," he says in a subdued voice.

I look at him, stunned. "What? Why...?" My voice falters. "Why would you say that?"

He doesn't respond.

"You love baseball."

"Maybe I don't anymore!" he snaps back. "Maybe I want to quit!"

I take a step toward him. "What do you think Dad would say about you quitting?"

The look on his face makes me sorry I said that.

I let out a deep breath. In a quieter voice, I ask, "Why would you want to quit something you love doing? That you're so good at?"

He doesn't answer. I stare at him. Is this part of his being mad at me? Does he think by saying this, he's getting back at me somehow? Maybe it's working. My stomach is doing flip-flops.

"I don't believe you," I say finally.

Silence.

"Talk to me."

"Leave me alone," he says.

"Not until you talk to me."

Face in the pillow again.

"I'm not leaving this room until we talk. You're ten years old. You're old enough not to hide in a pillow!" I pull it out from under him and hurl it across the room. It hits the door.

I hear movement in the hall outside. Mom coming out of her room from where she's been listening, probably. Is she coming to intervene?

"I don't believe you, Devon!" I'm afraid to hear the answer, but I push anyway. "You tell me right now what it is that's making you act and talk this way—"

"*He might have shot you!*" Devon shouts.

I stare at him.

"You could have been *killed*! *Just like Dad!*"

The movement in the hallway stops.

"Just like Dad…"

Devon is sobbing uncontrollably now, and with the pillow across the room, he cries facedown into the sheet.

I stare at him for what feels like a long time before I finally sit on the bed and try to pull him to me and wrap my arms around him.

"You shouldn't have gone down there."

"Devon—"

"You could have been killed!" he shouts. Over and over. "You could have been killed!"

And now he's hitting me, strong for his age, all those home runs he's hit, his fists pounding my chest and shoulders. It hurts. But I don't stop him.

When his punches begin to weaken, I try gathering him into my arms again. He lets me this time, and I hold him as tight as I can. "I'm sorry, Devon," I tell him. "I'm so sorry. But it's going to be okay now. I'm safe. You're safe. Nothing more is going to happen."

He cries, and I hold him, and we stay that way for a long time. I hear nothing in the hallway. Has Mom returned to her room, or is she listening from the other side of the door? Finally, I let go of him, and he sits up, wiping his face, wet and streaked and still dirty from the game.

"Is it true?" I ask again in a soft voice. "What you said about not wanting to play baseball anymore?"

"I miss Dad," Devon says. Simply, quietly. "I want him here."

My heart feels like it's breaking as I fight back my own tears. "I miss him too, Devon."

"Sometimes I forget," he says after a moment. "I'll make a good play or hit a home run, and I'll look for him in the stands because I want to see him cheering for me. Then I remember he's dead, and he's never even seen me hit a home run. He never will."

"But Mom and I are there."

"But what if you're not?"

"That won't happen."

"Dad should have shot the man!"

I pull back.

"He should have shot the man! He didn't have to put his gun down."

"He...he didn't want the girl to get hurt."

"I don't care. I wish the girl were dead!"

"You don't mean that—"

"Yes, I do! Dad was supposed to play ball in the backyard with me when he got home. We were gonna work on my hitting. After I did my homework. I was working really hard to get it finished so I'd be ready when he walked in the door. But he...he never did. He should have just shot the man. Why did he try to save her?"

"It was his job—"

"I hate him!"

The twisting in my stomach grows tighter.

"You don't—"

"Yes, I do. He got himself killed and he was supposed to come home and help me!"

"Devon—"

"I *hate* Dad!"

I don't know what to say to him. My insides feel tight enough to explode. The walls of Devon's room feel like they're closing in around me, and I have to get out.

"Maybe you should just…relax now." I fight to keep my voice under control. "Play with your DS or…something."

"I'm going to sleep."

Usually he fights it when it's time to go to bed. Yet here he is, before his normal bedtime, ready to close his eyes. He's still in uniform. He should get a shower.

"Sure," I tell him. "It's okay."

He turns onto his side and closes his eyes. Normally, I would stay and rub his back until he falls asleep. But I stand up, anxious to leave. I don't even pause to tell him good night.

Mom is waiting for me in the hallway as I come out.

"Damn you!" she hisses.

"What?" I say, shocked.

Angry tears streak her face. "How could you upset him like that? Make him say he hates his father?"

"Mom, I—"

"I told you to leave him alone. He just had a bad game. He just needed to be alone. But, no, you had to go in there. You had to *push* it—"

"I'm going for a walk," I announce, sidestepping her.

"You do that!" she snaps behind me as I head down the stairs, trying not to run but hurrying just the same as I head out the door.

20

NOW

"Why'd you stop?"

I'm still in the moment. The look on Devon's face. The disappointment in my mother's eyes.

"Chris."

I had started walking in no particular direction, thinking maybe it was better if I didn't come back. Mom and Devon both better off without me.

"Chris!"

"I blew it," I hear myself say.

Derek hesitates. "Blew what?"

"I thought I could be... I thought I could take care of him."

"Devon? Sounds to me like you're doing a pretty good job." He actually sounds sympathetic, which surprises me.

"I don't do enough. He needs..."

"Your father?" Derek finishes for me.

I take a deep breath and nod my head.

"Sounds to me like you've tried your best."

"But it's not *enough*. No matter what I do—"

"You're not his father."

"I know that."

"Do you?"

I look at him. "It's my job."

"What does that mean?"

"I have to protect him. Keep him safe. I've known that since Dad died. Mom said it herself. It was gonna be especially tough on Devon because he was only seven."

"You don't think she meant—"

"Being there for Devon was more important. It *is* more important!"

"More important than what?"

I don't say anything.

After a moment, Derek says, "It sounds to me like your brother looks up to you. That he really loves you."

"I let him down."

"How?"

"I should never have gone downstairs. I should have just called the police right away. I could have been killed. And now he's worried. Scared."

"Of what?"

"It happened to Dad. And it almost happened to me. Maybe he thinks it could happen to *him*. He's only ten; he's not supposed to worry about stuff like that. But maybe he's right."

"Right about what?"

"What do parents say? 'Don't worry. Nothing's gonna happen.' They promise that. But they can't promise it. Nobody can. Because we don't know. We *can't* know. We *can't*. How do I know my mom's not gonna walk in front of a bus tomorrow? Or Devon? No matter what I do."

Derek seems about to say something more, but he hesitates and leans back instead. Neither of us says anything for what seems like a very long time.

Why am I telling him this? What is he going to do with this information? What the hell does he want from me? I'm so tired of this, and, in some ways, I feel worse now than at any moment since I woke up here. Now I'm angry, and I'm wondering why he isn't threatening me with the shears again.

"What happened when you went back in the house?"
he asks instead.

Like he really cares.

21

THEN

After going back inside, I find a note from Mom stuck to my bedroom door.

I'm so sorry. If I'm asleep when you come in, wake me so we can talk.

I glance inside her room. She's lying in bed, mouth open, snoring quietly. I start to turn away, then notice the thin trail of smoke rising up from a dish next to her on the nightstand. I walk over and grind the cigarette into the plate.

I decide to let her sleep. She has the right to lose control sometimes. It must be hard raising two sons without a husband. Devon seems to be asleep as well. From the dim light supplied by the hall bathroom, I see him lying on his side, eyes closed, his Phillies bedspread pulled up tight around him, the way he always does no matter what the room temperature.

I turn away.

"Chris?"

His voice is so soft I wonder if I really heard it. But now I see him looking at me.

"Yeah?"

"I'm sorry."

I sit on the edge of the bed. "For what, kiddo?"

"For what I said."

I give him a smile. "You have nothing to be sorry for."

"I don't want to quit baseball."

"I know that. You were upset, that's all. Hey, you're still in the playoffs. Next game, I think you'll do great."

He doesn't say anything for a full minute. I'm waiting for that steady breathing to tell me he's fallen asleep when he says again, in a tear-tinged voice, "I'm sorry."

"I told you, you have nothing to be sorry for."

"But it was my fault."

I feel my stomach clench. "No, Devon. It's not. I told you—"

"You told me to stay in my room and I didn't."

"It's all right."

"I've been mad at you for going downstairs, but I did the same thing."

"Devon—"

"I was scared. That's why I yelled."

"Yelled?"

"I'd been looking for you and said your name. If I hadn't done that, the guy wouldn't have turned. And you wouldn't have to—"

"That's enough, Devon!" My heart is pounding. "What happened is not your fault. Do you understand me? Look at me!"

He looks up.

Seeing the expression on his face sharpens the pain in the pit of my stomach. "Do you understand me?"

"I lied to the police."

"Devon—"

"I told them I wasn't in the kitchen. That I stayed in the living room—"

"I know. We talked about this."

"They don't know—"

"Devon! It's better this way. As far as the police are concerned, you weren't in the kitchen; that's why they didn't ask you about what you saw. To them, you weren't involved except from the other room."

Tears are streaming down his face. "If I hadn't called out—"

"It doesn't matter. This is not your fault. It's *my* fault."

Devon says nothing for a long moment. Then he looks at me. "I lied to Mom."

I hesitate. "Devon, it's better if she—"

"Please don't tell Mom! I don't want her to know I lied. Please…"

"Of course I won't," I tell him, wrapping my arms around my little brother, who's already had to deal with more than any boy his age should have to. Holding him as tight as I can, I know there's no way I'm going to put him through anything more because of my actions. "I won't say anything," I tell him. "We'll keep it between us. It's over, Devon. The police aren't going to question me anymore. It's been ruled self-defense. It's over."

I continue to hug him until he says, "I didn't mean what I said about Dad."

I pull back and look at him. "I know."

"I don't hate him."

"I know you don't."

"Do you think he knows?"

Suddenly, my chest feels heavy, and it's difficult to talk. "I'm sure…I'm sure he knows."

"I miss him," he says. "I miss him a lot."

"I do too," I whisper.

"I don't want anything to happen to you too."

"It won't."

"You promise?"

"Yes. I promise."

Wiping his face, he pulls me toward him and says, "I love you, Chris."

"I love you too, Devon," I tell him, hugging him fiercely. And I do love him. So much it hurts. Certainly nothing could hurt more.

Except losing him.

22

NOW

"Devon was in the kitchen with you?" Derek says in a quiet voice, though sitting up straight now.

"Yes," I say after a moment. "I didn't know he came in behind me until he called my name and your brother turned and…"

"Why didn't you want to tell the police that?"

"I wanted him involved as little as possible," I tell him. "It was bad enough. He shouldn't have to—"

"It was because he saw it, didn't he? He saw you shoot Caleb. He saw that my brother didn't have a gun and you shot him anyway."

"No, that's not true."

"Yes, it is. I knew there was something." Derek leans in. "That's what you're trying to hide. You knew Caleb did not have a gun, but you shot him anyway. Killed him. Your brother knows that, and you don't want him telling the police!"

"No."

Suddenly, Derek presses harder on the garden shears, and I cry out.

"I told you I wanted the truth. Only the truth!"

I'm sweating, and my heart is beating so hard against my chest it hurts, and the sharp pain in my finger is intense and threatening to grow worse any minute. "Don't you think I knew how it would sound to you if I told you this just now? But I did it because you said you wanted the truth. That I *had* to tell the truth or..." I falter, but then manage to hold his gaze as I hiss through clenched teeth, "If you really believe I'm lying, then go ahead and cut my finger off! Just get it over with!"

We remain this way for a long time, staring at each other, as I wait for sudden, excruciating pain.

But instead, he eases the pressure and pulls the garden shears away. This time, I can't help showing my relief. Looking down, I see a fresh trickle of blood.

"What would your brother tell me he saw if I just asked him?" Derek says.

I don't answer—what's the point? I've gotten this far. If I can just hang on a little longer...

Derek does nothing. Doesn't move. Only stares at me.

Finally, he leans back and waits for me to continue.

This time, he keeps the garden shears in his lap as I go on.

23

THEN

The next morning, Devon seems better, though after our conversation last night, I find myself keeping my eye on him as the three of us have breakfast in the dining room again, even though the kitchen has been thoroughly cleaned. Even the bloodstain on the counter is gone.

A couple of times I think I catch Devon eyeing me, as if to say, *Remember, you promised not to say anything.* But I'm not going to tell Mom or Detective Fyfe or anyone. If he wants to talk with me about it, he can. But the fact that he lied about being in that room will remain our secret. He's been through enough. We all have.

Mom has made a good breakfast. Pancakes, Devon's favorite. He's always had a healthy appetite, and today he eats his usual four, a good sign. I eat my usual one. He still wants to walk to school alone. This time I get a hug, and I feel a little pain in my chest as I walk him to the door and watch him head up the sidewalk alone. But it's different this time. It feels good.

"You think he's okay?" Mom asks as I come back into the dining room. "I thought I saw him giving you a couple of funny looks there."

"He's fine," I tell her a little too quickly. She frowns, and I add, "We talked some more last night after I came back in."

"Why didn't you wake me?"

I shrug. "You were sound asleep. I didn't want to disturb you."

"What I said to you was horrible," she says, "and I'm sorry. I had no business… It's just I heard what he said about your father, and I was telling myself if you hadn't pushed him… I don't want Devon to hate him."

"He doesn't," I assure her. "He misses him. That's all. After what happened the other night, he's worried that the same thing that happened to Dad could happen to me. Or you."

"Jesus," Mom whispers. "I thought after three years, maybe…"

"He's okay now," I tell her.

"He certainly seemed okay just now," she says. "It must have been a good talk." She pauses then smiles. "You're so good with him. You're a better parent than I am."

"Mom."

She holds up her hand. "It's true, whether you want to admit it or not. I put too much pressure on you, expect more of you than what's fair. You've given up so much to be there for him. But things are gonna change around here. It's my turn to be the parent. Your turn to be a teenager. You're going to that party Saturday night and I'm watching Devon. You got that?"

My initial reaction is to object. But after thinking about it—especially imagining walking into that party with Rita next to me—I smile. "Thanks, Mom."

"What is that grin?" she says. "Do you have a date for this party?" When I bow my head, she pokes me in the shoulder, grinning herself, and says, "You do, don't you? Who is it? No, don't tell me. You just have fun."

Why not? I ask myself. *Always having to take care of my little brother. Put him first. Mom's got this. Saturday night I'm putting myself first and having a good time with Rita.*

When Devon gets home in the afternoon, he seems

even better. More relaxed. As if our conversation last night released such a burden from his shoulders that he can now be his old self again. And any other concerns I have are wiped away by the game he has Wednesday night. It's the second round of the playoffs, and Devon has one of his monster games. His biggest ever. Facing the Mariners again, who beat us to get the second seed, Devon goes five for five with three home runs, one of them a grand slam, while knocking in nine runs in a game. The White Sox win easily, 12–2, putting them into the finals, a best of three series, starting Saturday.

The team is ecstatic, the boys all jumping on each other in celebration, forming another big pileup.

It's the happiest I've seen Devon in a long time.

24

NOW

"Wait a minute," Derek says, straightening. "I just thought of something. Something you said earlier…"

I wait. At least he's not putting the garden shears back around my finger. He holds them loosely in his right hand.

"You said there was a certain way your brother looked at you during that game when he let that pitch go by and took the strikeout. You said it was the third time you had seen that expression on his face. The second time was just before he knocked over the catcher coming home."

My heart is back to pounding hard against my chest.

He leans forward. "When was the first time?"

"I...I don't understand what—"

"When was the first time you saw that expression on his face?"

"I didn't say second or third—"

"Yes, you—"

"No," I say, cutting him off. "You must have misunderstood me. Or maybe I just said it wrong."

Despite the pounding in my chest as he stares at me, I hold my gaze on him. We remain that way for a long time. Even with my arms and legs aching because of how long I've been in this chair, and my butt is long past sore to numb, I manage not to avert my eyes. Maybe I'm getting good at this, because all he does finally is shake his head and wave his hand. "Go on."

I close my eyes briefly before I continue.

25

THEN

Thursday night, after putting Devon to bed, I lie in my room and allow myself, for the first time in a few days, to think about the conversation I had with Derek Brannick at the ball field this past Monday.

I pull the card he gave me out of my wallet. Just a business card for some stupid-sounding clown who does birthday parties. I stare at it for a long time. I can hear Detective Fyfe's voice in the back of my mind.

Don't even think about it! Tear it up right now and forget about it. Move on with your life.

Maybe it's too late in the evening to call.

Tear it up!

I put the card back in my wallet.

I'm still thinking about it when I wake up Friday morning. Now that I don't walk Devon to school anymore, I don't have to get to school until homeroom. It's not like I have any extracurricular activities to get to. Mom now leaves before I do, so I have a little time to myself. I tell her good-bye and wait until the car is out of the driveway and down the street before pulling the card out again. Take out my cell phone.

What do you think you're doing?

I dial the number on the card. Bring the phone to my ear.

Glancing out through the front living room window, I can see it's going to be another gorgeous day. The weather forecast earlier said warm but not a lot of humidity. The same for tomorrow, good weather for Devon's game.

After four rings, I expect a voice mail to come on, but it doesn't. After eight rings, I'm thinking maybe I dialed the number wrong and I should try again. After ten rings, I'm thinking I should take it as a hint and forget all about this.

I put my finger on the disconnect button.

"Hello?" a voice on the other end answers. Rough, hoarse. And sounding annoyed.

"Derek Brannick?"

A pause. "Yes?"

"This is Chris Russo."

Another pause. Then, "You decided to call."

"Yes," I say.

"I'm glad." A pause. "To be honest, I wasn't expecting it," he says.

For just a few seconds, I panic. Detective Fyfe is right. I should hang up.

"So...how do you want to do this?" I ask.

"What day is it today?"

"Friday." It sounds like I've just woken him up or something. *Doesn't he have school like I do? No, I guess not.*

"What about after school? We can pick a place."

"I have to get home to my brother."

"Your brother...right. I read in the local paper he had a big game the other night."

Silence.

"I guess I could meet you for about a half hour," I offer. "If that's enough time."

"Whatever you can give me. Really. I'd appreciate it."

More silence.

"There's a Wendy's and a McDonald's right next to each other down the street from the school," I tell him. "I can meet you at one of those."

"Wendy's sounds good."

"There are a lot of people in there at that time of day," I feel the urge to add.

An awkward silence. "I'll see you then. I really appreciate this." Abruptly, he hangs up.

I look at the phone in my hand, wondering what it is I've just done.

———

I don't tell anyone what I'm planning, of course, not even Terry. I've been thinking about meeting Derek Brannick after school all day, feeling more and more nervous about it. My hands shake a little as Terry and I go through the cafeteria line. Rita and I have been sitting together during lunch these last few days, while Terry insists he sit somewhere else. But what if she can tell how nervous I am today and asks me why? I see her sitting by herself, looking in my direction, expecting me to come over. I hesitate, then feel myself start to turn the other way. "Aren't you sitting with Rita?" Terry asks.

"I...I don't have to," I tell him. "I thought I'd sit with you today."

"Yeah right," he says with a smirk. Then he looks at me, and I can see him about to ask if I'm okay. But he stops himself. "You're still taking her to Matt's party tomorrow night, right?"

"Right."

"Well then, get over there." He gives me a friendly push, then heads off to join a group at another table. I walk over and sit next to Rita.

"Terry could have sat with us," Rita says.

"I think he knows that." I arrange the food on my tray, reaching to open my milk.

"It looked like you weren't going to come over."

"No. I..." I almost drop the milk carton. "I was just talking to Terry."

She stares, as if studying me. "Are you nervous about the party tomorrow night?"

"No."

"I told you, if you ever wanted to talk..."

"Yes, you did. I'm sorry."

"It's all right if you are," she says.

"Okay. Well, yeah, I guess I am a little."

"That's fine. Actually, I like that you're kind of shy."

"You think I'm shy?"

"Unassuming then. That was a word in the vocabulary test today, and it definitely describes you."

I look down at my food, not sure what to say.

"Hey, that's a good thing," she says. "A lot of guys

around here, if what happened to you happened to them, they'd still be bragging about it big time." Suddenly, she shakes her head and says, "Look at me. I said I wouldn't talk about it and here I am doing just that."

"It's okay."

"No, it isn't." She looks at me again. "Are you having second thoughts?"

"Second—?"

"About taking me to the party?"

"No! I was thinking about my mother. She really might need me."

"I thought she was taking your brother to a movie."

"She is." God, I sound like an idiot. But I don't want to tell her the real reason why I'm nervous, that I'm meeting Derek Brannick in a few hours and the fantasy I've been having about him pulling a gun on me, no matter how crowded the Wendy's might be. "I just—"

"Because I've been thinking," she says. "We don't have to go to the party at all."

I look at her, surprised.

"If all everyone's going to want to do is talk about, you know, then maybe we won't go at all. We'll just go to your house, order pizza or something, watch our own movie."

Her hip touches mine. I feel my heart pounding. "I think Matt's expecting me to be at his party."

"So what?"

I open my mouth, close it. "You're right," I say. "So what? We'll go to my house." She smiles and starts eating her lunch. Rita can make something as simple as chewing look sexy.

Later, when the end-of-lunch bell rings, Rita says, "I'll see you after school."

"I...I can't," I stutter. "I've got something..."

"Your brother?"

"I, uh, have to meet him at his school for something then walk him home. Normally, he gets a ride with a neighbor." I hate lying to her.

"Okay. I understand." She seems disappointed. But then she brightens up. "Tomorrow night then."

"I'll walk over to meet you. If you don't mind the two of us walking back, I mean."

"Sounds fun."

I'd like to think that just being with her like this is enough to make me stop worrying about the meeting after school.

But it isn't.

26

NOW

Derek is shaking his head, a sneer on his face. "What a coward," he mutters.

"What—?"

He cuts me off. "All this talk about taking care of your brother, how important it is you be there for him, all the sacrifices you've made."

"I didn't—"

"'I was thinking about my mother. She really might need me,'" he says in a high-pitched voice, mimicking what I told Rita. "You were trying to get out of taking her."

"I was nervous—"

"About meeting me, yeah, I get it," Derek says. "But maybe nervous about going out with Rita too, huh? So you try falling back on your old excuse. *My mommy needs me to watch Devon.* Only this time you can't use it 'cause Mommy's got other plans. I swear to God, I don't know how you got the courage to ask her to that stupid dance in the first place. She was right to tell you no."

For the first time, real anger is overpowering this knot of pain I've had since I first woke up in this dingy room, and I blurt out, "You don't have the right—!"

"Oh, are you really going to bring that up again? Tell me what *I* have the right to talk about?" I expect him to produce the garden shears again, but instead, he just stares at me, as if I'm an animal he's studying in a cage. "You tell yourself your brother comes first, and it's okay. Poor you. But really he's just an excuse. An excuse to hide behind, so you don't have to *do* anything or take any risks."

Suddenly, in that singsong, high-pitched voice, made worse by its roughness, he mimics me again. "I can't go to the party. I've got to take care of my brother. I can't do things with my friends. I can't sing in the choir. I've got to take care of Devon. I can't have a life except for going to my brother's dumb baseball games because my daddy died and I've got to take care of—"

"Shut the hell up!" I shout. "That's enough!" To my surprise, he laughs then seems about to cough again, but this time he manages to stop himself.

"Now, now," he says in what is the closest to a playful tone he can probably muster, "remember the rules." He holds up the shears, smiling. "Truth," he says, "always truth. Admit it"—his voice gradually increases in volume and tension—"you didn't just decide to start taking care of your brother because of any obligation to your dad. You also did it so you could hide from everybody else, and it took you killing my thirteen-year-old brother to finally get yourself out of your shell!"

If I say what he wants me to say, what happens next? Is this what he's been looking for? A reason his brother is dead that goes beyond the simple fact he broke into our house? Will I be off the hook if I just *admit it*?

Maybe I should, but I tell him, "No!"

I'm glad they're starting that fall league and Devon's going to get a chance to play baseball some more.

"You're wrong. I love my brother."

You wait and see. Your brother's hitting is going to get a lot better.

"I'd do anything for him."

When he starts getting hits, they're gonna be monsters.

"Anything."

"Anything, huh?" Derek says. "But why? Because you love him? No. It's because you've always resented him, and now you feel guilty about it."

My stomach flip-flops. But I refuse to answer and hold his gaze. Whatever he's going to do, I want him to just do it!

After a while though, he finally sighs and says, "I'm going to give you a break about that one. If you're able to lie to yourself like that, then I guess I can't blame you for lying to me. So keep going."

27

THEN

The Wendy's is not as crowded as I thought it'd be. Five or six people are all. I was hoping for more—witnesses, just in case—if I was going to sit with the brother of the boy who died on my kitchen floor. Terry had something after school, so I didn't have to lie to him about not walking home with him. *What if Rita stops by the Wendy's though, sees me, and realizes I lied to her?* I look back, expecting to see her walking by at that moment. I tell myself to calm down.

It might have been better if I had come up with an excuse to stay home from school after making that call this morning. I left two homework assignments at home that were due today. In two different classes after lunch, teachers had to ask me the same questions several times before I heard them. I had to make additional stops at my locker because I'd grabbed the wrong book for class. By the end of school, I wasn't even sure I could make my legs work.

Derek Brannick is already here, sitting in a far corner booth with a Coke in front of him. He hasn't noticed me standing at the window. I reach for the door to pull it open and hesitate. No, it's more like I can't get my arm to move.

What the hell am I doing here? To talk to this guy about his brother? Why, to make him feel better? How can I do that? I certainly didn't know Caleb Brannick before he came into our house, and I don't know anything more about him now. What about making myself feel better? Will I stop feeling guilty if Derek Brannick tells me he forgives me, that he understands why I went searching for a gun before going downstairs? Do I even have the right to expect that?

No, this is stupid! Detective Fyfe has told me again and again. Nothing will be accomplished by talking to the family. His brother is dead. It's not my fault he broke into our house. Had a gun. What were we supposed to do? We have the right to protect ourselves.

Talking to this guy is only going to make things worse. Things are changing. Devon seems to be doing better. Life is improving. Rita is going out with me this Saturday. A month ago, if that had happened, I'd be ecstatic. Don't I have a right to be happy now? Don't I have the right to move on?

I back away. Derek Brannick still hasn't noticed me.

I let out a deep breath, trying to relax.

This is the right decision, I tell myself as I walk away. *Detective Fyfe is right; it's time to move on.*

I'm sorry his brother was killed, but I can't help Derek Brannick.

I can't.

28

NOW

"So you were there," Derek says. "You just decided not to come in."

I don't say anything. What's the point now? If I'd gone in there, talked to him, would that have been enough? Would I not be here now if I had?

I wait for him to say something, but he doesn't. Instead, he puts the garden shears in his lap and covers his face with both hands. I wait for him to say something, but he doesn't.

Finally, I take a breath.

This time, I don't need him to tell me to continue.

My story's almost over anyway.

29

THEN

Saturday morning, I take Mom to work; she tells me not to worry about picking her up, she'll get a ride to the game from one of Dad's old cop buddies who frequent the diner. Devon's awake by the time I return; he's so excited about the game, I don't get a chance to go back to bed.

I try to calm him down with a game of PlayStation *MLB*. I'm excited too, thinking about my date with Rita tonight.

After a while, Devon and I go outside and throw a ball around. We're not outside five minutes and Brady comes over, and the two of them throw to each other in the backyard. "Don't overdo it," I remind them. "Save some for the game."

Inside, the phone rings. It's Terry.

"Brady's at your house, right?"

"He and Devon are in the backyard."

"Man, I can't get him to calm down. They should have scheduled the game for nine o'clock. Make sure you send him back before ten. My parents have got some kind of errand to run before we head over to the field."

"Okay."

"What time do you think you and Rita will get to Matt's party?"

"We're not going."

"What do you mean you're not going?" Terry says.

"My mom's taking Devon to a movie, so we're thinking of just coming here to my house, getting a pizza, and watching a movie ourselves."

There's a long silence on the other end. Then he says, "You're gonna get some tonight, aren't you?"

"I...I don't know."

"Boy, when you make your move, you move fast."

"It was her idea."

"Even better."

"We still might come by—"

"Don't come by on my account. Go for it. But I want all the dirty details later."

"Come on, Terry."

"Didn't I tell you everything about Allison and me last summer? You owe me. Later."

I hang up the phone, a ridiculous smile on my face.

It gets to be ten thirty. Brady left a little before ten. Devon stayed outside, throwing the ball against the wall, a constant beat that I've long grown used to.

It's a little early, but I call out, "Do you wanna get your uniform on?"

As he races upstairs, the phone rings again.

"Hey, there, what 'cha doing?" It's Rita.

My ridiculous grin returns. "Getting ready to take my brother to his game."

"After you drop him off, you want to swing by and pick me up?"

"Swing by?"

"Mom and Dad had something to do this morning. I'm here by myself. I thought maybe I could go with you to watch his game."

My heart beats faster. The thought of her sitting next to me on the bleachers watching the game, with people seeing us together, both excites me and scares me for some reason. "Sure," I say. And just saying that makes my grin even bigger. Spending part of the day with her, then seeing her again tonight, just the two of us here at my house—this day is looking better and better. I deserve a day like this after everything that's happened.

Devon comes racing back down the stairs, his equipment bag on his shoulder. "Let's go!" he says.

"Shh," I tell him, indicating the phone in my hand, then ask him, "You got your water bottles?" As he hurries into the kitchen, I say into the receiver, "I've got to get Devon to the field by eleven."

"Can you come get me first then take him to the field? I'd like to meet your brother."

I'm not ready yet though. Which means by the time we'd pick her up, Devon would be late.

Devon rushes back from the kitchen. "I'm ready."

"Hang on a minute," I tell Rita, then looking at Devon, I inform him, "We've got plenty of time."

"I want to go now."

"I've still gotta get myself together."

"I can walk."

"Huh?"

"I wanna go now. I'll walk."

I look at him. "No, that's all right. Just give me a few—"

"I'm walking to school now. I can walk to the field."

"I guess if Brady wants to walk, you could go together."

"They already left. They had to go do something first."

That's right. I'd forgotten. But he's right. The Little League fields are only a couple blocks from the elementary school, so the walk wouldn't be much more than when he walks to school. And walking means he'll be there in time and I'd have time to pick up Rita.

"Chris?" I hear from the other end of the phone.

"Sorry. I'm dealing with Devon. Just a minute." I cover the receiver. "You sure walking won't tire you for the game?" I say to Devon.

"Chriiiissss," Devon complains.

"Okay," I relent. "Why not? Let me give you my cell. You can call me when you get there."

"Okay."

"Wait a minute." I'm not thinking. I'm not going to be here. "I'll call Terry on his cell a little after eleven. He should be at the field by then. He can tell me you're there."

"Why can't I call you here?"

"I'm...picking a friend up. Someone who wants to see you play."

He seems a little confused by that, then gives up and shrugs. "I gotta get going."

"Be careful," I tell him.

"I will."

"See you soon."

He waves and, pushing the screen door open, jumps outside and starts off down the street. I go to the door and watch him till he's turned the corner and gone out of sight. All he has to do is make one more turn, then it's a straight shot past the elementary school and on to the fields.

"I'm back," I say into the phone.

"Everything work out okay?" Rita says. Does she sound a little annoyed?

"Sorry it took so long," I tell her. "My brother's walking to the field. I was seeing him out the door. I'll come right now."

"I'll be waiting."

Five minutes later, I've changed and brushed my teeth, and I'm out the door and getting into the car. It's beautiful outside. Warm. Perfect for baseball. Perfect for feeling good about things.

I've thrown on a jacket, though the weather certainly doesn't call for it. I thought it'd be classier if I were dressed a little better than I'd typically be for a Little League game.

I get to her house in less than ten minutes. No car in the driveway. Like she said, she's home alone. There's plenty of time before the game. Maybe we can hang out here a little before leaving.

I get out of the car and take a minute to calm down. I don't want to come off as too jumpy or nervous.

I walk up to the door and knock. Nothing. I wait. For an insane moment, I wonder if it's possible I'm at the wrong house. I'm about to knock again when I hear from above my head, "Chris?" I look up and can't see her as she calls down, "I'll be down in a minute."

"Okay," I say. At first I'm not aware of my foot tapping as I wait. Then I realize I should call Terry, make sure Devon got to the field.

As I'm dialing, I hear the sound of footsteps coming downstairs. Rita on her way to open the door. What would she think if I tried saying hello by kissing her? *No, don't. Not yet. Keep cool.* I hear Terry's phone begin to ring on the other end.

All at once, it sounds as if her footsteps are behind me. Moving quickly. But I hear her calling from inside the house, "Coming!" Sounding happy. Happy to see *me*.

The pace of the footsteps increase and, confused, I turn around in time to see a figure fast approaching, reaching toward me with something in his hand. Instinctively, I try to duck.

And suddenly I'm in the dream.

"Shoot him! Shoot him!" I'm screaming at Dad. But Dad's moving toward the girl instead, so I lunge for Dad's

gun on the floor because if I can get to it before the guy fires, maybe I can save him. Everything's in slow motion. The guy's about to shoot...

Only it's not a gun, it's something else. A wet rag. Shoved into my face. Accompanied by a sweet smell.

I struggle, but my eyes start feeling heavy, and my whole body begins to weaken.

Is that the sound of the front door being opened? Rita's tentative voice? "Chris?"

Or maybe I hear Terry's voice on the phone, saying, "Hello? Hello? Chris, is that you?" before everything goes dark around me.

30

NOW

"Chloroform," Derek says, removing his hands from his face. He'd kept them there the whole time I was talking. The garden shears are still on his lap.

"What?"

"That's how I knocked you out. I put chloroform on the rag. Don't worry. There aren't any long-term effects."

I don't say anything. Now that I'm finished, I feel a kind of relief. He has to see now that doing this isn't going to accomplish anything.

I wait, wondering, *Are we finished now? Did he get what he wanted from me? Is he going to release me?*

All at once, he lurches forward with the garden shears and takes hold of a finger. Only, this time, it's the index finger on my right hand.

"If I asked you now whether or not you saw a gun in Caleb's hand, would you be able to tell me?" Derek asks, his rough voice low, hushed.

I look at him. "No."

"Are you at least sorry my brother's dead?"

"Yes! Oh God, yes!"

His voice continues in a soft whisper. "I thought talking to you…I might understand—even accept—what happened. But I can't. Not yet…"

It looks like he might start coughing again, but if he was he manages to stifle it.

"There's something," he says, "I don't know…something you're not telling me."

I've come this close. I can feel my nerves tingling, but I keep my voice steady as I say, "I've told you everything—"

"I'm going to ask you another question," Derek growls, "and I want you to think before you answer." Another cough, but he cuts if off, his breath hot and sour against my face. "Why did you take that gun?"

"I don't know. I wish—"

The shears flinch, like a living thing. "I *told* you to think."

"O-okay. Give me a minute."

I think back to that night. Waking up, thinking I'd heard something. Checking on Devon. Checking my mom's room too, seeing she wasn't home yet. I remember straining to hear more, some sign that someone might be downstairs but hearing nothing. If I called the police, and no one was there, I'd look stupid. I decided, finally, I should check. Just to be sure.

Then I remembered the gun Mom keeps in the side table next to her bed.

"Why did you take the gun?"

Unlocking the drawer, taking the gun out, feeling the weight of it in my hand. Thinking I should check to see if it was loaded, but not sure if I knew how. Though Mom had told me she always kept it loaded.

I remember that the sight of it was ugly. And I wondered if the guy who'd killed my father had done it with a gun like this.

And then just as it had that night, the dream comes back again, only this time I'm awake, facing Derek, but at the same time I'm reliving the dream, as if it's real, oh God, it feels so real…

"Shoot him! Shoot him!" I'm screaming at Dad.

"Please, please don't. Don't make me remember…"

"What?"

But Dad's moving toward the girl instead, and though I wasn't there when it happened, I am this time, so I lunge for Dad's gun on the floor because if I can get to it before the guy fires, maybe I can save him. Everything's in slow motion. The guy's about to shoot...

"Chris?"

...and my fingers encircle the gun on the ground, lift it, point it at the guy, who's now pulling the trigger...

"Chris." The blades tighten.

"Dad put the gun down. Why did he do that?" My voice sounds harsh, my throat hurts. Fresh tears are finding their way down my face. "I didn't mean to..."

...and I pull the trigger before he does, the gun going off, but now the guy is gone and in his place is Devon, and the bullet I've just fired is heading toward him...

"No!"

...but my father is moving, jumping in front of Devon, and the bullet that would have hit my brother, the bullet I shot, hits my dad, and he goes down, blood spurting.

"Chris, if you don't tell me—"

"I didn't mean to..."

"To what? Shoot my brother?"

"No. Shoot my dad."

"What? You didn't—"

"In my dream. He thinks I'm trying to kill Devon. I

guess because of what I said to him. But I wasn't. He jumps, and I hit him. Over and over again. Every time. I keep telling myself, if the dream can change, if he lives, then maybe it means he's forgiven me. For what I said to him..."

"You're not making sense. If you're trying to pull something..."

"I can't change anything," I say slowly, trying to make him understand. "That's what the dream means. He's dead. And I can't take it back. And I can't take back what I said, what I did. But I can protect Devon. Because it's what Dad would want. Protecting Devon, taking care of him, is more important."

I actually start coughing myself. When I'm finished, Derek says, "What can't you take back?"

When I don't respond, he says, "What do you mean by 'more important'?"

"It was going to be harder on Devon since he was only seven; that's what my mother said."

He says nothing.

"I had to take care of him. I have to *keep* taking care of him. It's what Dad would want."

"Are you saying you protect Devon because he was more important to your dad than you were?"

"Goddamn you, you're going to make me say it?" I

yell at Derek. "Yes! Of course, Devon was more important to Dad than me! Maybe he loved me, but not the way he loved Devon."

My voice chokes, making me stop. Tears have broken loose, running down my cheeks. I take a breath and struggle to continue. *You wanted the truth, Derek Brannick? Okay, you son of a bitch, here it is!* "Devon was the kid Dad always wanted. He's happy, well liked, gets good grades. He's an athlete. He was the son who loved baseball as much as him. Not me. Dad would try to get me interested, but I wasn't, not really. He would never say it, but I could see it in his eyes—how disappointed he was in me. But Devon came along, and they were always playing baseball together, talking about it. At first, Devon kept striking out or hitting weak ground balls. But that was okay with Dad. He'd just say, 'That's all right; he'll get it.' And he did. He figured it out. But not until after Dad died..."

I stop for a moment, catching my breath. The tears keep coming, and I've stopped fighting them. "I always told myself it didn't matter, that it was all right. And then...I couldn't help myself. That night, I just blurted it out. I don't know why. I didn't mean to. It just came out. I could tell it hurt him. But he had to go to work—he had a double shift—and I told myself I'd say I was sorry the next time I saw him...and then I couldn't because...because he was killed the next day. And I will *never* be able to tell him. So I thought the only...the only way I could make it up to him was to take care of Devon. To always be there for him."

I take a ragged breath, and Derek cuts in, saying, "You're talking about the last time you talked to your father?"

I look at him, hesitate. Then nod.

In a surprisingly gentle voice, he says, "So tell me, what happened on that walk?"

I've told him this much. I might as well tell him the rest.

31

THEN

It's late summer; school is starting in a week. Dad is talking about the Phillies. "Things didn't work out this year," he says, "but if they could just make the right move or two this off-season, they could be right back in the hunt, I'm telling you. Don't you think, Chris?"

"It'd be nice," I offer. He glances at me, his expression suggesting he knows I'm not really into talking about this, the way I'm not ever into talking about baseball, no matter how many box scores he read to me as a baby. But tonight I have some good news to tell him, something I'm really excited about.

"Dad, the choir director at school called me today. She wants me to try out to be one of the soloists for this year. Remember I had that real short thing I sang in the concert last year?" Actually, Dad missed it because of another double shift. "She said she thought I had a beautiful voice. I should try out. It'd be a real honor if I got picked for that. If I get it and then sing well enough this year, I might even be able to try out for regional choir. The ones who get that are considered the best middle school singers in our part of the state."

"That's nice," he says after a minute. "I'm sure you'll... When are the tryouts?"

"Right after school the second day."

Dad pauses before responding. "I think...yeah, I think Devon will have tryouts for the new fall baseball league that day, to see what team he's gonna be on." He looks at me. "Your mom and I don't have to be at your tryouts, do we?"

"I...I don't know... I don't think so."

"That's good," he says. "Hopefully, I can switch shifts with somebody that day, so I can take Devon to his tryout."

"I'll need a ride home after—"

"I'm glad they're starting that fall league," Dad

continues, not hearing me now, "and Devon's going to get a chance to play baseball some more."

Has he ever heard me? Maybe he stopped after it became obvious baseball was never going to be my thing. Certainly he stopped after it became clear Devon could be molded into the perfect son after Dad failed with the first one. "You wait and see," he's saying. "Your brother's hitting is gonna get a lot better. His bat's slow right now because he's so big for his age, and he's still getting used to his own body. But one day, maybe in fall ball, maybe next summer, the light's gonna go on, and then, watch out. When he starts getting hits, they're gonna be monsters."

We're almost to the police station when he looks at me and says, "We'll all three want to make sure we get to Devon's games, even if it's just a fall league. It'll help him with his confidence to see us cheering for him. You especially, being his big brother."

We stop at the main entrance to the station. "I'll just get one of the guys getting off shift to take you home," he says, reaching for the door.

I want to try telling him one more time: regional choir! It would be a really big thing. It'd be important. It would make *me* important!

Instead, I hear myself say, "I can walk home."

"No," he says, "Come on in with me. I'll ask—"

"Shit, Dad, I'm thirteen years old. I can walk home by myself."

Where did that come from? I never curse in front of my dad.

He looks at me in disbelief as, he says, "Chris, you know better than to talk like that."

What I should do is apologize. What comes out instead is, "I may not be able to hit home runs, but I can certainly walk six goddamn blocks by myself!"

Now Dad is staring openmouthed at me, probably wondering where this strange alien who has taken over his oldest son's body has come from. "I don't know what is going on with you, but we'll talk after I come home tomorrow, I promise you that. Now come in here with me and I'll get someone to take you home."

I need to take back what I said, and I try to get control of myself. But I hear myself stumbling over my words. "I...I'm sorry, Dad. I don't know what... Look, don't worry about the solo tryouts. I can get a ride... I'm not even sure I'm going. It's not that important..."

"Well, apology accepted," Dad says. "There's never an excuse for cursing at your father. But, Chris, I didn't mean you shouldn't..."

I want him to continue, to hear what more he was

going to say, but now he's looking at his watch and telling me, "I don't want to be late; we'll talk about this when I get home. We'll talk to Devon too, double-check when his tryouts are—"

"Screw Devon!" I shout, like a bomb just went off inside me that I couldn't disarm. "And screw *you*!" And with that, I start walking home. I keep expecting him to come after me to at least make me apologize for defiling the great Devon's name and insist I wait for one of his cop buddies to drive me home.

But he doesn't. I just keep walking, and it isn't until I'm inside our house that I can think back to the look on his face just before I turned away from him, a look that says maybe I've done something irreparable. And I start counting the hours until he is home from work and I can apologize for what I've said and make things right again.

32

NOW

A long silence follows. I feel exhausted, wasted. My eyes are closed, so I don't see the expression on Derek's face, though I feel the shears in place around my index finger.

Finally, I hear him say in that uniquely soft, rough voice of his, "Why did you quit choir again?"

Surprised, I open my eyes. "After what happened, I needed to be there for Devon. And choir wasn't a big deal."

"Stop telling yourself that," he says, cutting me off. "It was a big deal." He leans in. "The truth, remember?"

After a moment, my head down, I whisper, "Yes. It was."

"You should have tried out," Derek says. "You let your father take that away from you."

Fresh tears have formed in my eyes. I should say something, but I can't.

"And that's the last you saw of him?" Derek asks. "That was the last conversation you had with him?"

I nod, still looking down, feeling dull and lifeless. "I wanted to apologize, to tell him I don't know why I said that to him, that I didn't mean it."

"But instead he screwed up your chance to apologize by getting himself killed."

I hesitate, then nod again.

"I'd say he deserved you getting angry at him."

"No, he didn't! I loved him. And he did love me."

"As long as Devon came first, right?"

"I shouldn't have said it. Now I can never apologize."

"And even worse, he never got the chance to apologize to you. Did you ever think of that? Who knows? If he had come home the next day, he might have told you *he* was sorry. In my opinion, he should have. But I guess you'll never know."

After a long moment, Derek says, "Well, well, the truth has come out." He lifts up the garden shears. "No matter how much I threatened you with these, you were holding that back." He leans in. "Makes me wonder what else you might have held back."

"N...nothing," I whisper.

I know I should be fighting back more, telling him, yes, this one thing, yes, that was all, it's all out now, I'm sorry. But it feels like I've been in this chair for so long, I'm not sure what's real and what's not. And maybe I don't care anymore. If he said he was going to cut off two fingers for lying to him, I'd raise up my hand—if I could—so he could get to them easier and get it over with.

But the shears remain where they are, and he studies me.

And then when I think it's finally over, all at once he leans forward and says, "Let's try it again, shall we?"

I look at him.

"My brother was robbing you, right?"

"I...yeah, I guess." I'm so exhausted.

"You *guess?*"

The sudden anger in his voice makes me sit up. "He was in the kitchen," I tell him. "The cabinets were open."

"He was probably looking for food. He'd been living on the street. He was hungry."

"The police said there were other break-ins in the neighborhood."

"And I bet if you checked out what was actually taken,

you'd find out it was mostly food. Caleb was trying to survive."

He pauses, lost in thought.

I try to swallow; it hurts.

"Let me get you some more water," Derek says, getting out of the chair. Moving behind me, out of sight. Like before, I hear the squeak of a faucet turning on, water running, then the faucet turning off.

He comes back into view, cup in hand. "Tilt your head back." All of the water makes it into my mouth. I swallow, grateful.

Again, he crumples the cup and tosses it on the floor. "Better?"

"Yes," I answer. "Thank you."

He sits back down, looks at me. "I'm supposed to believe that you weren't sure whether or not my brother was holding a gun."

"It's true. It was dark. It looked like... I reacted."

"You and I both know you saying that means nothing now. I don't know if I can believe you."

Abruptly, Derek gets up and starts pacing, waving around the shears. "It was probably a loaf of bread. Or a can of soup. But you pulled the trigger."

"It was a gun," I say.

"Why? Because the cops told you?"

Fiercely, I nod my head.

"There's no way Caleb would've had a gun. No way. He was getting food, that's all. Maybe a little cash if he'd found some. He was living on the street, for Chrissake. No way did he have a gun."

"He did," I hear myself say.

"I know you need to tell yourself that to feel better about what you did. But it doesn't make it true."

I know what he's getting at, but I don't want to admit it. "You're wrong. The police, they—"

"They *planted* it!" Derek shouts.

And there it is. Out in the open. What I didn't want to admit. What's been nagging at me ever since Detective Fyfe spoke to me in the police station.

"What, you think the police never do stuff like that?" Derek seethes. "They come to your house and find a scared teenage kid, the son of a cop who died in the line of duty, who'd just killed an intruder for doing what? Pointing a can of soup at him? No way were they going to let that stand. Of course they planted the gun. It was easy. Everyone goes home happy. The son of a hero gets to be a hero—protecting his brother, his family. Just like his father would have done. Makes for a great news story. And so what if the victim was some homeless thirteen-year-old kid breaking in just 'cause he needed to eat."

Then, in a softer voice, Derek says, "Of course they planted the gun."

He turns his back to me.

"You don't know that!" I hear myself blurting out. Knowing I shouldn't, that I might be, yet again, putting myself in more danger by doing so. But I can't help myself. "You're just telling yourself the police planted it because you don't want to admit that your brother had turned into a criminal while you were in prison. Oh, excuse me, 'juvenile detention.' You're just trying to ease your own guilt. You're mad at me because I *protected* my brother. And you *didn't* protect yours."

I wait for him to do something. Anything. He barely moves. After a while, maybe I hear something. Could he be crying?

My arms, back, and legs ache from not being able to move. I have to go to the bathroom. I can hear my own harsh breathing. I wait for him to turn on me, the garden shears waiting to strike!

But still he doesn't move.

After more time passes, I'm not looking at him anymore. I'm seeing Caleb Brannick, his back to me, only dim light coming in through the window from a streetlight outside; he suddenly turns around at the sound of Devon's voice, and seeing his hand, his right hand, coming toward me, I strain to see what's in it. I work to slow it down, freeze-frame it, and as it comes into focus, I begin to see...

All at once, Derek moves, wiping his eyes as he turns to face me. The shears are still in his hand, though they hang by his side. He looks defeated. Worse than when he first appeared in this room with the weight of the world on his shoulders.

He sits in the chair. Leans forward again. I watch the shears, but they do not come up.

"I want you to understand this is nothing personal," he says. "It's not about revenge. It's about balancing things out. Making things right."

What's that supposed to mean?

"We're all victims here," Derek says. "My brother. You. Me. There has to be a way..." He hesitates again. Another long silence.

What more does he want from me? What more?

All at once, he scrapes the chair forward so that our faces are now only inches apart. "I forgive you," he says. "I understand what happened and why you did what you did..." He falters, looks away for a moment. "I forgive you. But that doesn't mean no one pays." He pulls back again. "I need to check on something. And I need a little time to think."

Abruptly, he brings the shears up, and I pull back. But he uses them to cut through the duct tape wrapped around my chest. Then he cuts and pulls the tape from around my legs. Before starting on my wrists, he looks at me.

"There's a cell phone for you by the door. Do not leave this room until I call you. I'm not going to be far, so if you try to leave before you hear from me, I'll know. And you won't like the consequences, believe me." He pauses. "Do not call *anybody*. Do you understand?"

"Yes," I say.

He holds the shears poised above my wrists. "Don't try anything." Then, quickly, he snips at the duct tape, freeing my hands. Then he pulls back. I rub each wrist, sore from the pull of the tape. But, otherwise, I don't move.

"Remember, don't leave until you hear from me." He stares at me another few seconds, then nods and moves.

I don't look back to watch him leave. When I hear the sound of the door closing, I let out a long breath. After that, I finally stand.

My knees are stiff, and I wobble and sit back down. My hands are shaking, and I drop my head, taking in more deep breaths. After a few minutes pass, I get back up again and, this time, manage to stay on my feet.

Turning, I can see the whole room now. Hard,

concrete floor. Rough walls. It's a laundry room. A utility sink sits in the far corner. A few paper cups are stacked next to the faucet. On the wall next to the door, a washer and dryer sit next to each other. On top of the washer is the cell phone Derek was talking about.

I see my jacket crumpled on the floor; I grab it, I slip it on, then cross to the door. Hesitate before turning the doorknob a little. It's unlocked. Every bone in my body is telling me to get out of here.

I'm not going to be far, so if you try to leave before you hear from me, I'll know. And you won't like the consequences, believe me.

They could just be words to try and keep me here. Or he could be right outside, checking on whatever it is he needs to check. *Using the time to think*, he said. Think about what? How stupid I am sitting here, afraid, while he's running off somewhere?

I cross to the washer and pick up the phone. It's on. The clock's not set, so I still don't know what time it is.

For all I know, he's not going to call. His threat was just a ruse to get me to stay here. But why leave the cell phone unless he really was going to call? Otherwise, I could use it to get help.

I should call the police. But I don't know where I am, and tracing a cell phone call could take longer than I can keep the phone open. What happens if he calls me right in the middle of it?

You won't like the consequences, believe me.

I lay the phone back down. Stare at it. *Ring, damn it! Finish doing whatever nut-job thing you're doing and call me. I'm sorry your brother's dead, but he shouldn't have come into my house with a gun. And don't tell me you know for sure he didn't have one.*

The phone just sits there.

You won't like the consequences, believe me.

Silence. Nothing.

How long have I been here? How long was I unconscious before I woke up? Could it be nighttime? Or even the next day? Are the police looking for me?

I figure I only have time for one call. I should call Mom. Even though I couldn't tell her any more than I could tell the police, I could reassure her at least that I'm alive. Do I call her cell or the home phone?

But what if I wasn't out that long? Could it be earlier than I think? Is it possible Devon's game could still be going on, with Mom watching, wondering where I am but not worried about me yet? She usually leaves her cell in the car at Devon's games, so what if she doesn't have it with her in the bleachers and I've wasted my one chance?

And I can't help thinking about Rita opening the door when he grabbed me and wondering if Derek hurt her. I need to know she's okay. If I call her, find out she's fine, I can get her to call Mom. Then get right off. I'll be quick.

But what if she's not okay?

Damn it, make a decision!

The cell looks pretty straightforward, easy to dial. I dial her number. Wait. One ring. Two. Three. Come on, *answer*!

Four. It stops. A female voice. "Hello?" Not Rita's.

"May I speak to Rita?"

"This is her mother. Who am I...speaking to?" Something in her voice.

"Uh...Matt." *Stupid. Why did I say that?* She'd recognize his voice, wouldn't she?

"Oh, hi, Matt." She's obviously distracted. "She's..." Hesitation. "I'm sorry. She's...had an accident."

Oh my God! "What happened?" I ask. "Is she... Is she going to be all right?" This is already taking too long.

"Wait, you're not... Who is this?"

I hear a beep. The sound of someone calling in.

I panic and hang up on Rita's mother. Switch to the other call. I've blown my only chance. But did I switch fast enough that he didn't notice?

"I'm here," I say in a low voice.

There's a long pause. Does he know I was on the other call? Is that why he's not saying anything?

So what if he does know? What's he going to do?

You won't like the consequences, believe me.

"So have you finished *thinking*?" I ask, cutting into the silence. Now that he's not here with his shears, I feel stronger. If he suddenly came back into this room right now, he wouldn't be facing the same scared teenager.

He doesn't respond right away. Maybe I pushed him too much. So what? I should hang up on him, just open that door, and step outside.

"It's good that you're angry," I hear him say. "You're going to need it, I think." A deep breath. "There's something you have to do. Go to Detective Bob Fyfe. Get him to admit that the gun was planted. Record it for me, so I can hear him saying it. You do that, and we're finished."

I actually take the phone from my ear and look at it in surprise. When I bring it back, I hear him saying, "I can't get close to him. But you can. And this is going to be good for both of us. You'll know the truth. As I know it. I brought you a small tape recorder you can use. Just make sure it's hidden somewhere on you, so he can't see it when you get him to talk. And if you're thinking about going to the police about me—"

"Wait a minute," I cut in. "What makes you think I'll—?"

"I've got your brother."

I stop. Suddenly, the room I'm standing in seems to pull away, leaving only me and the phone and Derek Brannick's voice on the other end.

"You're lying..." My voice falters. "You don't have—"

"When you let him walk to the game by himself, I was watching. As soon as you closed your front door, I grabbed him."

"I don't believe you. You're just saying that to—"

A sound on the other end. The phone shifting. Then a different voice comes on. Familiar. Scared. "Chris?"

Devon's voice.

"Come get me. Okay? Chris, please?"

I feel gut punched. I open my mouth to respond but can't breathe or talk.

"Chris?" His voice is so small.

"I'm coming, Devon," I manage. "You hang in there. Okay? I'm—"

The sound of the phone on the other end moving again. Then Derek's voice returning. "*Hang in there. That's the same thing I said to *my* brother.*"

"You son of a bitch!" I snap through gritted teeth. "Let him go. He has nothing to do with this. Nothing—"

"I'm doing this for both of us," Derek says, his voice remaining maddeningly calm. "You should know that." He pauses. "I'm sorry for what I just said. That crack about you telling your brother to hang in there… That was cruel."

"If you hurt him—"

"You'll what? Come after me? I don't think that would be a fair fight. I'm not planning to kill him, if that's what you're worried about. But if you don't follow my instructions, then I'm going to ask him what happened. What he saw. There's still something you're not telling me. So if I ask him, what's he going to tell me? That you knew Caleb didn't have a gun and shot him anyway? And if he won't tell me right away, I'll hurt him. I'll start with one arm. I'll break it in several places. He loves baseball, right? Probably dreams of being a professional baseball player when he grows up, and unlike most kids his age who have that dream, he actually has the ability to make it come true someday maybe, right? I'm sure your father dreamed that for him. But I wonder if after his arm healed, he'd be able to play baseball the same way again."

Now the room has closed in on me—again. I fight to breathe.

"Are you listening?" Derek asks.

"Yes."

"Good. Once you go outside, you'll see that you're in a house. This neighborhood is only a couple blocks from where I grew up, actually, and only a few miles from where you live. If you go in the garage, you'll see a car. It belongs to the couple that lives here. They're an elderly couple that go to Florida every winter and won't be back for a week or two. Keys are in the ignition. The tape recorder I talked about is in the glove compartment. There's also a gun, loaded. Six bullets. In case you need an edge to get Detective Fyfe to talk. I should also warn you, your mother called the police hours ago, so they're looking for both you and your brother; you'll have to be careful."

"I can't just..." I hear myself say. "Fyfe isn't going to just..."

"I know this is a shock," Derek says. "And it's going to be difficult. But it has to happen this way. I'm sorry. You'll be highly motivated, so be creative. You said you'd do anything for your brother. I'm giving you the chance to be a man of your word."

"Please, don't do this," I whisper. "It won't bring your brother back."

Silence. Then I hear, "Don't you think I know that?" Another pause. When he speaks again, his typically harsh voice has turned colder, darker. "After—" He coughs. "After you've gotten his confession on tape, call me on the disposable phone. The number's programmed in there. At that time, I'll tell you where I'm holding your brother. Now you better get moving. It's almost seven o'clock. You've got until eight."

"One hour? I can't—"

"Yes, you can. I have to put a time limit on it, so you'll continue to appreciate the urgency. Don't call me until you have the recording. If I don't hear from you when time is up, you might as well not call. But I promise for the next hour, your brother will be safe."

"Please..." I try one more time. "Come after me but don't hurt him."

Silence on the other end. Then, in a voice so low I almost can't hear it, Derek says, "It's more of a chance than you gave my brother."

The line goes dead.

One hour.

Phone in hand, I open the door.

33

NOW

He didn't say anything about me being on the phone when I called, so maybe he doesn't know. Or maybe he doesn't care, knowing it will be over in an hour one way or another. Might Rita's mother call the police about the strange phone call she got? Could the police put two and two together somehow and figure it was me? But why would she bother? She just thinks I'm some anonymous jerk who called.

Rita. What did Derek do to you?

An accident, her mother said.

I can't think about that right now. I've got to focus

on rescuing Devon. If he can hurt Rita, he's capable of following through on his threat to Devon.

Outside, I find myself in a backyard. I see the garage, but first I head around to the front to get my bearings.

A neighborhood, just like he said. Houses similar in style, one right after another. I see two people sitting on their front porch a few houses down. No one else seems to be outside. In every way, things appear perfectly normal. Serene.

It's still warm, but the sun is low. Dusk will be coming soon.

I've got to get moving.

The garage door opens easily. The car is there. The keys in the ignition. The clock inside actually says it's 6:55. Okay, I have an extra five minutes. Matt's party starts in about an hour. Is he still expecting me to show up with Rita to tell my story? Does he know what happened to her? Maybe she's in the hospital. Wait a minute. If the police are looking for me, is it possible that the police think I hurt Rita?

Concentrate. In the glove compartment, I find the tape recorder and pull it out. I stare at the gun also sitting in there and leave it inside.

The urge is to start the car, peel out of there. Rush, hurry, drive fast. But what would that accomplish? I can't just go running into the police station and into Detective Fyfe's office. Even if they don't think it was me who hurt Rita, there'll be questions. Answering them will take time. And do I really expect Detective Fyfe to tell me, even if we're alone, that they planted the gun under Caleb Brannick's body? What if the truth is, he didn't? What if Derek is wrong? How will he react? What will he do to Devon?

Time seems to be ticking away inside my head like a bomb, but I have to slow down. I have to force myself to think.

One hour. Why just an hour? Surely he knows it's impossible. Maybe he's planned all along to get back at me for killing his brother by hurting mine. But he wants to play with me first. Torture me. Make me think I have a chance when really I don't.

I'll start with one arm. I'll break it in several places.

Oh God. I close my eyes, concentrate.

Maybe I could bluff him. Wait till just before a quarter to nine to make it more believable, then tell him I've got the recording. Just so he'll tell me where he's holding Devon.

But he's probably thought of that and will insist on listening to some of the recording on the phone first.

I could try faking the recording. Do it myself, pretending

to be Detective Fyfe. It might be enough to fool him over the phone. Get him to tell me where Devon is.

And I've got a gun. Once I'm there, I'll make him let Devon go. Shoot him if I have to.

But he's bound to have a weapon himself. There's too much of a chance of Devon getting hurt. Even killed.

God, poor Devon. He must be so scared. Counting on me to save him.

I'm your big brother. I will always be here to protect you.

Why did he give me a gun?

In case you need an edge to get Detective Fyfe to talk.

Does he really expect me to pull a gun on a police detective? Even if doing so got him to talk, how would I know he was telling me the truth? With a gun on him, he might just be telling me what he thinks I want to hear.

Maybe there's more to why he gave me a gun. But what?

I can't think about that right now. He's given me a chance, as small as it is. I've got to take it.

Focus.

You said you'd do anything for your brother.

Focus!

I'm giving you the chance to be a man of your word.

When the plan suddenly comes to me, my eyes fly open. Could it work? I think it through. Maybe. It's all I have. It *has* to.

The clock on the car's dashboard reads 7:00. Exactly one hour.

I need to get out of here before neighbors begin to notice the garage door is open to a house where the owners are supposed to be out of state. I start the car and begin to back out slowly. No need to attract attention by speeding out of here.

I turn onto the street, facing north. I notice a neighbor across the street stepping out of his front door, looking at me curiously. The garage door is still open. I'm not going to bother getting out to close it. I head off down the street. Looking in the rearview mirror, I see the neighbor crossing the street to the house I just came from.

To follow through on my plan, I need to make a stop. A mile down the road and to the right, I pull into a Walmart. The clock reads 7:05. I hurry in. Fortunately, I find what I'm looking for near the front of the store. Tiny blessings.

I pull out of the parking lot at 7:13. Before doing so, I took the card Detective Fyfe gave me the night we spoke outside the police station out of my wallet. His personal cell phone number is on the back. I punch in the numbers.

It starts to ring. What if he doesn't answer? *Stop thinking like that. He* has *to answer.*

Four rings. Five. Six.

His voice mail's going to kick in any minute.

Seven.

"Bob Fyfe."

Not a recording.

"Detective Fyfe? It's Chris Russo."

"Chris, where are you? We've been looking for you."

I hear the urgency in his voice and imagine him signaling people around him.

"I didn't hurt Rita. I didn't—"

"We know."

"Is she okay?"

"She's in the hospital with a fairly serious concussion. She was unconscious for a while, but she woke up a little while ago. They're going to keep an eye on her, but her prognosis is good."

I take a breath. "I need to see you. Just you. Right away. Otherwise, he's going to hurt Devon."

"You mean Derek Brannick?"

Hearing the name surprises me, and I falter, my planned speech flying out of my head.

Detective Fyfe jumps into the silence. "A number of people saw him talking to you at the game last Monday," he says. "Somebody we talked to after you went missing actually got him in a photo he was taking of the boys on the field, which helped us identify him. But truth is, we considered him right away. Haven't been able to find him. His parole officer didn't even know where he was. So we figured it had to be him that took you and Devon."

"You knew about him being out?" I hear myself say. "And you didn't warn me?"

"We were keeping an eye on him."

"You did a great job of that, didn't you?"

"Chris—"

"I'm gonna be in front of the Memorial Park sign in two minutes," I tell him, getting back on track. "I'll wait five. No more. If you don't show up, or I see other police in the area, I'll leave, figure something else out."

"You don't have to—"

"I only have until eight o'clock. So just do what I say. Please."

"Chris, listen—"

I cut him off by hanging up. Slip the cell phone inside my jacket.

Either he's going to be there or he's not.

Before moving, I pull the gun from the glove compartment and slide it into my jacket.

The clock reads 7:22.

34

NOW

Memorial Park is two blocks down the street from my house. The dashboard clock reads 7:24 as I pull up half a block short of the sign, which sits close to the road. I leave the car idling, hunching down low in the seat.

I only gave him a total of seven minutes to get here, so he wouldn't have time to set up anything. No time for any kind of wire surveillance. But I'm not naive. The police will try something. I pick the cell phone up off the seat next to me and wait. I tap my right foot on the floor.

Three minutes. My right foot keeps tapping. I flip the

phone back onto the seat. It bounces and almost falls to the floor.

Four minutes. Now my fingers are tapping on the dashboard. I pick the phone back up. Quickly put it back down. If he doesn't show, what do I do? Call Derek and beg? Call Detective Fyfe back and tell him everything, hope that, somehow, they can find Devon in the little time left? Maybe I should have called the police right away. Let them do what they're trained to do.

Five minutes. I decide to wait a little longer. Tap tap.

Six minutes. The phone is back in my hand.

I see him hurrying up to the sign, looking for me. I see no car by the curb that he could have gotten out of. I doubt he walked here. He would have had to run in the time I gave him, and he doesn't look out of breath. Somebody drove him, another cop probably. Someone who dropped him off a block away, maybe, so I wouldn't see him, and is now looking for a place from which to keep an eye on us.

Pulling up quickly next to Detective Fyfe, I call out, "Get in!" through the open passenger-side window.

He looks surprised; he didn't expect me to be in a car. "Now!"

He hesitates.

"Fine," I say and take my foot off the brake.

"Okay, okay," he says, yanking open the passenger door and climbing inside.

I pull away before he's closed the door, drive three blocks, then turn into a shopping center parking lot, pulling around behind the row of stores and stopping. Maybe I shook the other car, maybe I didn't. But if it's close by, I doubt it will come back here and risk being seen.

I shove the gearshift into park. The clock reads 7:34.

"Open your shirt," I tell him.

"I didn't have time to put on a wire."

"Do it!"

Detective Fyfe unbuttons his shirt, opens it. I'm not sure I know what I'm looking for, but nothing looks suspicious. Of course it could be someplace else on him, but I don't have time to check. I'll have to trust that he's telling the truth.

From under the seat, I pull out the tape recorder. "If he doesn't hear from me in about twenty minutes that I've got a tape recording of you admitting you planted the gun on his brother, he's going to hurt Devon. Bad. He says he won't kill him, but I don't know if I believe him. He thinks you planted the gun to protect me. He wants the truth." After a moment, I add, "*I* want the truth."

I hold the tape recorder up and make a show of pushing the record button.

"This is Chris Russo. I'm talking to Detective Bob Fyfe of the Maple-Braden police force. Detective Fyfe, identify yourself."

Detective Fyfe says nothing, scowling at me.

"Detective Fyfe, I'm asking you, did you or another member of the police force plant the gun found under Caleb Brannick's body the night I shot him?"

He still says nothing.

"Detective—"

All at once, Detective Fyfe grabs the tape recorder from me and turns it off. "You don't have to do this, Chris."

"Give that back!"

"You don't cooperate with someone like him. You think if you show up with my voice on this tape recorder, he's going to let your brother go? More than likely, he'll kill both of you. You want to help Devon, you tell me where Derek Brannick's holding him, where it is you're supposed to meet him after you make this tape."

"It's too risky."

"And what you're doing isn't?"

I lean in. "You told me if I needed anything from you, to call. You said you'd be there for me. Well, I need something now. I'm desperate. Please help me."

He stares at me. I see anger in his eyes.

The clock reads 7:42. *Hurry up, damn it!*

His expression changes. He looks at the tape recorder in his hand, then emphatically pushes the record button and begins to speak into it in a harsh, edged voice.

"You want the truth?" he says. "On the night Caleb Brannick was killed, a gun was discovered under his body during the course of the on-scene investigation. Further investigation over the next couple of days confirmed that the gun belonged to one Helen Brannick, Caleb's mother. When we talked to her, Mrs. Brannick said she had only noticed the gun was missing in the last month or so—this was confirmed by a police report she'd filed—and before then, she hadn't even taken the gun out of the closet, where she kept it in a shoe box, in ten months or longer. Since it turned up in her son Caleb's possession, it was determined that either he had taken it without his mother's knowledge when he ran away from home or that, at some point later, he snuck back into the house to steal it. The truth is he had the gun on him the night he broke into the Russo home and was killed. His death was caused by an act of self-defense. Case closed."

Detective Fyfe angrily turns the tape recorder off and extends it toward me. "If you want to go play this for him because you think that's the best way to save your brother, go ahead. Or you can tell me right now where it is you're supposed to meet, and we can go get him."

When I don't take the tape recorder from him, he puts it away in his jacket pocket.

"You won't have enough time," I tell him.

"You'd be surprised."

I swallow, take in a deep breath. "I'm supposed to meet him by the big roller coaster at the old amusement park that closed down five years ago."

"Fun Time Alley? In Ridner?"

"Yes."

Reaching inside his jacket pocket again, he pulls out a cell phone. "Got that?" he says into it.

"We're already on our way, sir," a voice from the phone answers back.

"Good. Keep me apprised."

I stare at him. "Someone was listening the whole time?" I say. "I didn't even think of a cell phone."

"We usually know what we're doing."

"What if they don't get there in time?"

"We can move fast when we have to. Plus, they'll be getting the Ridner police involved as we speak. It's going to be okay."

Tossing out those words like it's that easy. *It's going to be okay.*

"I wish you'd called us right away when you had the chance."

"I'm sorry. I should have."

Detective Fyfe sighs, putting a hand on my shoulder. "You were trying to save your brother. You thought you were doing the right thing.

"Where'd you get this car?" Detective Fyfe asks.

"Derek left it for me to use."

"Derek? You're on a first-name basis with him?" He looks at me then mutters, "Stolen, probably."

I don't say anything.

"We got your car from the front of the Moyer home, by the way. We'll get it back to you soon, get you a loaner in the meantime. Found your cell too."

I just nod.

"Let me drive now. I need to get this car into impound for evidence, and we need to question you, but I know your mother will want to see you. I'll drop you home. There've been two officers with her, in case a ransom call came in. You can come by the station when we have your brother."

We switch places, and the car starts moving. I see the minutes clicking down as we pass Memorial Park, then the baseball field where Devon plays his games. Soon, we're in front of my house.

The sun has started to dip below the horizon, making everything around us turn a shade of gray.

"As soon as we've got him, I'll call you," Detective Fyfe says. "I promise."

I go to open the door, glance at the car clock. Nine minutes till eight.

My heart's pounding. But there's still time, and I have to be sure he's telling the whole truth. Devon's life may depend on it.

"When you questioned me at the station the night it happened," I say, speaking carefully, "you specifically told me not to mention to the assistant DA that I didn't remember actually seeing the gun in his hand. If you knew he had a gun, why was that so important?"

"Come on, Chris." He sees me staring at him, sighs. "I just wanted to make things easier for you. That's all. There was no need to complicate things."

"Complicate."

"Yes. Now, I really have to—"

"What is it you're not telling me?"

Exasperated now, he shakes his head. "There's nothing—"

"Yes. There is."

In a lower voice, as if he's afraid someone is listening, Detective Fyfe says, "Why can't you just drop it, Chris? With everything your family's been through—"

"If you don't tell me, I'm always gonna know there's something. I don't want to live with that. I'd rather live with the truth." I grab his arm. "Bob...*please!*"

After a moment, Detective Fyfe shakes his head again. "You are relentless, aren't you?"

I just wait. Heart now *slamming* against my chest.

Another moment passes before he begins. "Caleb Brannick definitely had a gun. Just like I said. The gun belonged to his mother, and he brought it into your house. But we didn't find it under his body. We found it in his pocket. So it couldn't have been in his hand when you shot him. We took it out and put it under his body, to make it look like he'd been holding the gun and dropped it, then fell on it."

I let his words move slowly over me.

It couldn't have been in his hand when you shot him.

"It doesn't change anything, Chris. You understand that, right?"

They come to your house and find a scared teenage kid, the son of a cop who'd died in the line of duty, who'd just killed an intruder for doing what? Pointing a can of soup at him?

"Are you all right?" I hear Detective Fyfe ask.

"Yeah," I say in a low voice.

"What I said about calling me if you need to talk...
That still goes."

"Okay."

"Go see your mother. She needs you. I'll talk to you
later."

I get out of the car.

It couldn't have been in his hand when you shot him.

*It doesn't change anything, Chris. You understand
that, right?*

But it does change things. In essence, the police did
plant the gun.

Derek was right!

And if I hadn't gone downstairs, an unarmed thirteen-
year-old boy would not have been killed.

"Are you sure you're okay?" I hear Detective Fyfe ask
from the car.

"It helps to know."

"Still, if you want to talk..."

I nod, and Detective Fyfe puts the car in gear, waving
as he pulls away.

I move slowly toward the house, listening for the
sound of the car to diminish behind me.

As soon as it's gone, I turn back toward the road,

just shy of the front door. As I begin walking down the sidewalk, I pull out the cell phone Derek had left me from my jacket, along with the second tape recorder I bought at Walmart. Thankfully, it's still running. I rewind it and listen to make sure I've got Detective Fyfe's voice clearly.

The clock in the car had read four minutes till eight when I got out. I'm in good shape. I got it all, and there's still time. Moving quickly, I push the button to dial the number Derek programmed into the phone.

Two rings. Three.

Pick up, pick up.

Five rings. Six.

Please, please, pick up.

Seven rings. Eight.

Why the hell aren't you—?

Suddenly, his voice comes on.

"You're too late."

And he hangs up.

"No. No! I'm not!" I'm shouting, even though I know he can't hear me. As I call right back, I yell, "I have a couple minutes!" It rings. Ten, eleven times. Nothing.

Then the ringing stops. Followed by a click that ends the connection.

I collapse onto someone's front lawn. It was all

for nothing. Derek had never intended to let me save my brother. Was he hurting him right now? *Devon, I tried. I—*

The phone rings.

"I've got it!" I blurt into it, wiping tears from my eyes.

Long silence. "You do?"

"Yes."

"Play it."

I bring the recorder up to the cell phone.

My desperate voice plays out. "*You told me if I needed anything from you, to call. You said you'd be there for me. Well, I need something now. I'm desperate. Please help me.*"

Silence. Then comes Detective Fyfe's voice.

"*You want the truth? On the night Caleb Brannick was killed—*"

I cut it off, bring the phone back to my ear.

"Keep it going," I hear him demand.

"No. I'll play the rest when I see you."

"You're in no position to—"

"Do you want me to play this whole thing for you? Then tell me where you are, where Devon is. I'll play it then. You know I will."

A long silence. Has he hung up? Did I push it too far? "We're at the baseball complex," he says finally.

"The minor field. Where we first met. I'll have him in the home dugout."

"Put Devon on the phone," I say.

"You'll see him—"

"I want to know he's okay. If you want to listen to this tape, put him on."

The sound of shuffling. Then I hear, "Chris? When are you coming?"

"I'm coming right now. I'll be there soon. I promise."

Derek comes back on. "Now get over here."

"It'll take a few minutes. I don't have the car anymore."

Another silence. "Ten minutes."

Then he hangs up.

I'm already running.

35

NOW

Saturday nights, the field complex is empty. Games are always finished by now. Kids come here to play on their own sometimes, but it's almost dark and no one is here. I'm carrying the tape recorder; the gun from the car is inside my jacket.

The minor league field is secluded from the others. I enter the field from the visitor's dugout side. A bright moon allows me to see Derek and Devon sitting on the bench in the home dugout. Devon sees me and starts to move. But Derek rises and presses the gun in his hand to Devon's head, holding him in place.

Devon looks scared but in control. Just thinking of what Derek has put him through today fills me with rage. I should have pulled the gun out before I got here. I picture myself firing it at Derek, killing him.

When I reach the third base line, maybe ten feet from the dugout, Derek tells me to stop. "Play it," he says.

I place the tape recorder on the ground before pushing Play and backing up.

Detective Fyfe's voice plays out loud and rough from the little box.

"You want the truth? On the night Caleb Brannick was killed, a gun was discovered under his body during the course of the on-scene investigation."

Derek doesn't move, does nothing except stare straight ahead as he listens to the rest of the tape, the gun still holding Devon in place. I wait, trying to catch Devon's gaze, wanting to impart the message with my eyes, *It's going to be okay. Just hang in there a little longer. It's almost over.* But his eyes are on the recorder, listening as well, eyes wide.

Nothing else around us seems to exist. Just my disembodied voice questioning Detective Fyfe's.

It seems to take forever, but finally, the tape ends with the detective's voice saying, *"Still, if you want to talk…"* Then comes the sound of the car driving off.

Followed by silence.

Carefully, I cross to the tape recorder, crouch down, and turn it off. "Do you want it?" I ask Derek.

He slowly shakes his head.

I step back, leaving the recorder on the foul line. Wait.

After a long silence, I hear him say in a low voice, "Nice touch. Sending them to the old amusement park. But by now, they've figured out you sent them on a wild-goose chase. I'm sure they're looking everywhere for you."

"I couldn't trust them," I say. "I couldn't make myself believe things wouldn't go wrong somehow."

The gun is still pressed against Devon's head. Devon's breathing has turned shallow.

It's almost over, kiddo.

"Why did he take Mom's gun?" Derek says. "He hated guns, he... Stupid."

"But he didn't use it," I say. "It was in his pocket. I shouldn't have..." My voice breaks, and I take a breath. "I'm sorry. I wish... I'm sorry—"

"It was *my* job to protect him," Derek cuts in. "I was his older brother. As soon as I could get out of that house, I did, and I just left him there, knowing what he was facing, alone, and I did nothing. I sacrificed my little brother." Now Derek looks at me. "I

would have done the same thing you did. Gone downstairs with a gun."

I stare at him. "I didn't have to," I say. "I could have
just called the police."

"Maybe. A bad situation though, either way."

A bad situation. Like my dad found himself in. If he
hadn't put his gun down, he'd probably still be alive.
But he saved the girl. He did his job. And if he hadn't
broken the policeman's cardinal rule and held on to his
gun, or hadn't jumped in front of the girl when the guy
fired, and the guy had killed the girl, would he have
been able to live with that? Everybody always says, "Do
the right thing." But sometimes the right thing just isn't
clear. Sometimes you just have to choose and then live
with the consequences the best you can.

The silence between us feels like the quiet before a
sudden storm. Or an explosion. The gun is still in place.
Devon still sits with his arms on his knees, waiting.
Waiting for his big brother to save him.

"You said you'd let him go," I say quietly.

Derek looks at me, shakes his head. "No."

"What?"

"This isn't over."

I take a step and he pushes the pistol harder against
Devon's head. Devon cries out.

"Don't... Please. I did what you asked."

"Yes, you did. Damn you!" he shouts suddenly, trembling now. "But you were supposed to fail. You *should* have failed! I only gave you one hour, an impossible task. People like to say, *It's going to be okay. I'd do anything for you.* It's bullshit. It's not possible." He shoves Devon again, using the gun. Devon winces. "I wanted to show *him* it's not possible. I wanted to show *you*. I wanted you to fail like *I* failed, so you'd know what it feels like to make a promise you know you can't keep and watch it blow up in your face."

My voice comes out tight with anger and fear. "And if I had failed, then maybe you could've justified leaving home, leaving your brother behind, told yourself it wouldn't have mattered. But I didn't. And if it makes you feel like more of a failure than you already are, well, I can't help that. I am not going to let you hurt my brother! If you want to get back at me for killing Caleb, then you do it to me. Not to my ten-year-old brother."

"No. That's too easy. Too noble."

"*What do you want from me?*"

"One more test. To see if you really mean it."

"Test? Jesus—"

"Do you have the gun I left for you?"

I hesitate. "Yes."

"Take it out. Slowly."

Carefully, I pull the pistol out, holding it so he can see it. Now he's probably going to tell me to toss it on the ground. It's just like Detective Fyfe said. He isn't going to let us go just because I did what he said.

"Come on. Grab it like you're gonna use it."

"What?"

The gun is shaking against Devon's head. "I'm going to kill him unless you stop me!"

"You promised—"

"*Point the gun!*"

I bring it up. My hand slick with sweat, I point it at him.

"I know what it's like to be pushed aside for someone else, the way your father pushed you aside. Once Devon was born—who was everything your father wanted in a son—he didn't want you anymore. You know that's true."

"My father wasn't perfect," I say quietly, intensely. "I know that now. But he loved me in his way."

"But you know he loved Devon more."

"Don't try to justify what you're doing by trying to make Devon and me like you and Caleb."

"I *heard* what you said to your father," Derek shouts. "I *saw* the look on your face when you were telling me the truth! The last thing you ever said to him before he died!" He indicates Devon with a nod of his head. "Now tell *him*! 'Screw Devon! And screw you!' That's what you said!"

Hot tears are filling my eyes. I glance at Devon then back at Derek. "Don't... Don't..."

"You've only been there for Devon since your father died because you feel guilty."

"That's not true. Don't listen to him, Devon. I love you."

"But at least your father died knowing the truth about how you felt!"

"He knows I was angry. But he knows... My father... knows...I loved him..."

"Shut up! No! You can't take it back! You don't know. You don't know what he thought."

Tears are streaming down Derek's face now as well. The gun is wavering slightly but still pointed at my brother. "You want to know the truth about my brother and me?" he says. "When I got older, my parents stopped wanting me. I'd gotten past the age where they wanted to love me anymore—their kind of love. The nights they used to come into my room—I hated it. My father doing whatever he wanted with me. My mother letting it happen. But at least I knew on those nights I was special to them.

"And then they didn't want me anymore. My father didn't... He wanted *him*. Caleb! They shut me out! So I know what it's like to hate my father for not loving me anymore! But the truth is, when I left, I left because I was angry at my *brother*. For taking them away from me. I tell myself now that I always planned to go back, that I was always going to get him out of there. Because I knew—I *knew* what they were doing to him. *Because they used to do it to me.* But when I left, I knew I was never going back. Even when he came to see me in prison and I told him to wait a little longer, to hang in there, I was angry because I was jealous! Isn't that sick? Oh God! I didn't leave because I hated my parents. I left because I hated *Caleb*! As if he had a choice in what they were doing to him those nights. I'm supposed to forgive what my parents did to me so I can learn to forgive myself. But how can I forgive myself for *that*?"

I stand there, horrified. The gun in my hand.

"Just like you, I told myself I would keep my brother safe, but I failed," Derek continues. "I let Caleb down in a way I'll never be able to repay. I wanted you to fail, but you didn't. You got that damn recording. But it doesn't work that way. You can't promise you'll keep the ones you love safe. Not unless you're willing to pay the price!"

He still holds the gun against my brother's head. "I'm going to prove it to you." Devon just stares, as if he's in shock. "You're not going to let me hurt him? You'll do anything to protect your brother? Here's a chance to prove to him you mean it. Show him how far you'll go. I'm not talking about how you say you shot Caleb; that was almost an accident. I'm talking about making a conscious choice on your part."

"But why?"

"*Somebody* has to pay for my brother!" Derek cries. "So you decide who it's going to be. Devon? Or me?"

My hand trembles as I point the gun, and I bring it down. "I...I can't..."

"You love him? You'll do *anything* for your brother? Go ahead. Show him!"

"Please don't make me—"

"I'm going to count to three."

"Just go. All I want is my brother."

"You're right! I'm a failure! So I need to pay for my brother's death, or you get to know what it's like to let Devon die when you know you could have stopped it. One..."

Again, I try to level the gun. My arm is shaking so much I have to hold it with both hands. What if I miss Derek and hit Devon?

"Two..."

"Shoot him! Shoot him!" I'm screaming at Dad. But Dad's moving toward the girl instead, so I lunge for Dad's gun on the ground...

I apply pressure on the trigger. But I can't seem to get my finger to move.

I try one more time. "Please don't—"

"Three!"

Neither of us is watching Devon, who may be ten but is big for his age and strong. Moving suddenly, he jumps up and drives an elbow into Derek's gut. Derek lets out a *whoomph*, falling forward, and the gun in his hand goes flying in the air, hitting on the dugout concrete then bouncing away.

"Run, Devon!" I shout.

But he doesn't run. Instead, he remains where he is, transfixed, staring at Derek.

Derek is on his knees, working to get his breath back. I look for his gun but don't see it. I put myself between him and my brother. I try to push Devon away, but he resists. "Come on, Devon. Come on!" He still looks like he's in a daze, but finally, he moves a few steps toward the other end of the bench.

Holding my gun on Derek, I tell him, "Get up." He does, breathing easier now, looking at me with a resigned expression.

Darkness has finished settling in, but the moonlight makes it easier to see.

It takes me only another few seconds to decide. "Go."

Derek's eyes open up. He doesn't move.

"I'll tell the police you listened to the tape, then left Devon with me and just ran off. I'll tell them I found your gun after you were gone; you must have dropped it. They'll be mad at me for sending them to the amusement park, but what are they gonna do? You should get going though. I'm sure they're looking for you."

Still, Derek doesn't move. "Why?" he asks.

"If you want to kill yourself, *you* have to do it. Not me." I take a deep breath. "And maybe I owe you. For your brother. For Caleb."

He seems to think about it. "I'm probably not going to get very far."

"Maybe...you could get some help. That counselor. Or talk to somebody else about, you know, what your parents did to you...and your brother."

"Yeah, right. No one's going to listen to me after what I've done."

"You better get going."

Derek ponders me for a moment. Maybe he didn't hear me.

"I said you better—"

Now, much to my surprise, he actually smiles. "You did a good job holding it back. But I know now the one other big truth you wouldn't tell me," he says.

My heart leaps. "What are you...?"

"You didn't shoot Caleb."

I feel my heart quickening. "Look, just get out of here while you can—"

"You don't have it in you. I was about to kill your brother. Who you said you would do anything to protect. But you couldn't pull the trigger. So I guess there *is* something you wouldn't do."

I stare at him, dumbstruck. Then, all at once, angry. I feel my finger suddenly tightening on the trigger. "You think I wouldn't—?"

"It's okay." He leans in. "I understand. I wish I had loved my brother as much as you love Devon. But you don't have to worry. Your secret is safe—"

The sound of a gunshot behind me catches both of us by surprise. Derek goes stumbling backward, and by the time he's on the ground, sprawled on his back, I can see the blood blossoming from a wound in his chest. Like I've imagined the wound that killed my father must have looked.

"*Nooo!*" I shout, rushing toward him, but I can already see there is nothing I can do. His eyes are wide and unseeing, and though his mouth is open, I can tell that it's not going to be like it was with his brother, who lived long enough to try and tell me something while the blood pumped out of him.

Derek is dead.

Wildly, I turn back to see Devon, my ten-year-old brother, standing there with the gun that Derek had dropped still smoking in his hand. "Devon, *drop it!*"

I recognize the look in his eyes—it's the fourth time I've seen it.

"You said there was a certain way your brother looked at you during that game when he let that pitch go by and took the strikeout. You said it was the third time you had seen that expression on his face. The second time was just before he knocked over the catcher coming home. So when was the first time?"

"I…I don't understand what—"

"When was the first time you saw that expression on his face?"

"Devon!"

The night Derek's brother was shot.

I remember the gun Mom keeps in the side table next to her bed. Unlocking the drawer, taking the gun out, feeling the weight of it in my hand. Thinking I should check to see if it was loaded, but not sure if I knew how. Though Mom had told me she always kept it loaded.

I remember that the sight of it was ugly. And I wondered if the guy who'd killed my father had done it with a gun like this.

"Devon, give it to me."

And I put it back in the drawer and closed it. Went downstairs without the gun. But I must have forgotten to lock the drawer. Which is how Devon got the gun. I didn't know he'd followed me until...

In a quieter voice, I say, "Devon, please."

"So when was the first time?"

...I heard the gunshot behind me, saw Caleb Brannick fall, turned, and saw Devon holding Mom's gun.

My brother finally looks at me, his eyes dead. As dead as Derek's had looked when he first walked in on me tied up. "Dad should have shot the man," he says in a cold monotone.

"Devon, Derek was leaving. You didn't have to—"

"Dad should have shot the man." All at once, my brother passes me the gun, the same way he did in the kitchen.

"Sit down," I tell him. He sits on the dugout bench.

I stand there, looking at him, thinking back to that night.

"Go into the living room, Devon. Wait for me."

After calling 911, I went to talk to my brother, who was sitting quietly on the sofa. *"Devon, why did you—?"*

"Dad should have shot the man."

"What?"

"Dad would still be alive if he had shot the man. If he hadn't put his gun down, he could have. You didn't take the gun. I had to."

A police siren begins to sound in the distance, and I know it's coming for us. Maybe somebody heard the shot and called it in. Or maybe people saw figures in the ballpark at night and thought they should report it.

We don't have much time. I have to do something.

Was Derek right? If Devon hadn't elbowed him in the stomach to get away, would I have just let Derek shoot him? I don't know. Maybe I'll never know.

Dad could have pulled the trigger, but he didn't. And he ended up giving his life for a child that wasn't even his own.

Devon was willing to pull the trigger to protect me. Twice. But was that really the reason? Jesus, what if he *saw* that Caleb wasn't holding a gun? What if he *knew* that Derek was going to walk away? And he still shot them?

He's only ten years old. He couldn't... He can't... No, Devon hadn't understood what he was doing. All he had known was that his brother was in danger.

I look at Devon to find something to reassure me,

some form of regret on his face. But he still bears the same blank expression.

He's just in shock.

Well, there's only one thing I know for sure. All this time I've been trying to protect my brother, and really, he's the one who's been protecting me.

So I can do this for Devon now. I can tell the police I shot Derek Brannick, just like I told them I shot Caleb. Later, I'll talk to him about it, when it's just him and me. I'll *help* him understand. Help him deal with it.

The sound of the police siren has grown louder. Devon seems not to hear it.

Time to act.

What I tell Devon is the same thing I said to him in our house that night.

"Devon, listen to me. We are telling the police I did this. Do you understand? I pulled the trigger. Not you. Do you understand?"

"Yes," he says simply. His expression remains the same.

Using my shirt, I wipe the gun clean then hold it firmly so my fingerprints will be on it. Then I place the gun on the bench next to me and finally take a breath.

This is the best I can do for now. But at least this time, I won't be doing it for my father. I'll be doing it for Devon.

A steady breeze has started coming in from over the right field wall. Over where Devon hit his last home run, one of three that game. He had been amazing that day.

"It's gonna be okay now, isn't it?" Devon suddenly says. "We're safe now?"

I put my arm around him and pull him close.

Now I see flashing lights appearing, heading toward the entrance to the ballpark complex.

Devon and I hold on to each other and wait for the police to arrive.

ACKNOWLEDGMENTS

It was a long time between novels, and there are so many I want to thank for this one.

First, a thank-you to Karter Huber, Luke Tomrell, Anne Huber, and Tracy Koontz for reading *The Truth* during its various stages and offering valuable input. I appreciate it so much.

I also want to thank my editor, Aubrey Poole. Thank you for your support and guidance in helping make *The Truth* the best it can be and for all you did in making the revision process fun and productive. I also want to thank the Sourcebooks team for all their help and great ideas (including coming up with a much better title than I did).

A big thank-you to my wonderful agent, Wendy Schmalz, for hooking me up with Sourcebooks. Thank you for the enthusiasm and support you showed for this novel right from the beginning. It came at a time when I really needed it. We make a good team, and thanks in large part to you, the future looks brighter than it has in quite a while.

Finally, all my love to my wife, Janet, and our son, Will. Your love and support mean so much. I love you both dearly.

ABOUT THE AUTHOR

Jeffry W. Johnston has published about thirty-five short stories and over two hundred articles. His first young adult novel, *Fragments*, was an Edgar Award nominee for Best Young Adult Mystery and a Quick Pick for Reluctant Young Readers selection by YALSA. He writes music, and plays guitar and sings in a band. He also loves watching movies, reading, and binging entire TV series. Jeffry lives in the Philadelphia area with his wife and their teenage son. His website can be found at jeffrywjohnston.com.